WHAT LURKS BETWEEN

MICHAEL KINGSWOOD

CONTENTS

ABOUT THIS BOOK

From a place beyond reality, it comes to consume the world.

For Barry, getting a transfer to a new position as an electrician aboard the Ketcham Space Station summed up his professional life perfectly: just one dead-end job after another. Little did he know that job put the fate of the world in his hands.

Waking up at home with no memory of how he got back from the Station, Barry soon finds that he brought something back with him. Something hungry. Now he has to stop it. Somehow.

Enjoy the book! After you're done, please come to Michael's website and sign up for his mailing list at michaelkingswood.com/newsletter-signup/. Guaranteed to be spam free, he uses it to announce new releases and special promotions for his fans.

WHAT LURKS BETWEEN

It came from outer space.

Well...sort of.

It actually came out of my lunchbox. But I brought my lunchbox into outer space that day, and trust me, it was *not* in that lunchbox before I went up. That's how come I can say it came from outer space.

What was it? Long story, but it starts simply enough.

So there I was, and this is a no shi-- Erm...sorry. That's the Navy in me coming out. But trust me, this really happened. Really.

Like I said, it started out as just another day on the job...

―――

"Barry!"

I turned away from my locker to see Clark Haberman, the very last person I wanted to deal with, walking toward me. As usual, he wore his light-gray work coveralls, cinched at the waist with a black web belt that supported a number of tool pouches, and a scowl on his weathered face. Christ, what had I done now? I couldn't think of anything I'd screwed up lately, but Clark never got that look except when something had gone seriously wrong.

"Yeah, boss," I said, inwardly wincing as I anticipated the diatribe to come. I was amazed when it never did.

"You've been reassigned."

I blinked.

"You hear what I said? You're not working here anymore."

So that's how it was. I sighed and lowered my eyes. I had been fired before, lots of times, but at least the other bosses didn't screw around trying to make nice about it. "We don't need you anymore." "You messed up one too many things." "Get lost, loser." I had heard them all. But never reassignment. That was rich.

I let out a bitter laugh before I was able to catch myself. From the corner of my eye, I saw Clark's eyebrows twitch upward in...confusion?

No way.

"I ain't joking, dude. They want you up on Ketcham Station, starting today."

Clark held out a printout as he spoke. Expecting yet another pathetic joke at my expense, I snatched it away and began reading. As I did, my bitterness and fatalism faded, replaced by amazement. And maybe just a smidgen of hope.

"Congratulations," the note began. I could not recall the last time anyone had congratulated me for anything. It continued, "Your application for service aboard the Ketcham Station has been accepted. You will begin work on 27 April. Report to shuttle station seven at 0930 for transport. Welcome aboard!" The note was unsigned, but it came on company letterhead, and the office code at the top indicated it was from Human Resources.

"I didn't apply for duty on Ketcham Station," I murmured.

"I applied for you," Carl said, his scowl becoming more like a sneer. "You're always talking about how you should have stayed in the Navy. Ketcham's a ship. Sort of." He cleared his throat softly. "Anyway, I figured it was time you moved on to something better."

Better. Right. The Ketcham Station was a hole, and everyone knew it. Old, dilapidated, and about ready to de-orbit any week now, if the rumor-mill was to be believed. So yeah, I *was* getting fired again. So much for that smidgen of hope.

Oh well. At least this time I got to keep a paycheck. And, truth be told, if Ketcham Station was as run-down as they said, it would probably have plenty of work to keep an electrician like me busy for a while. Maybe I could rack up some more overtime on this gig.

"Great." I tried to sound like I meant it. Then I saw the clock: 0900. The shuttle station was a twenty minute walk from the locker room. Crap.

Wasting no time on chit-chat, I turned back to my locker and pulled out my duffle bag. It did not take long to pack all of my stuff; I only kept my lunchbox, a towel and soap, and the clothes I wore to work - jeans, a t-shirt from a trip to the Alamo, and a pair of beat-up sneakers - in there. Other guys kept their lockers full; I guess I never expected to stay all that long.

"Well," Carl said as I packed up, "good luck up there. Been nice working with you."

I knew he was lying, but it was nice of him to say it. Maybe he wasn't a total schmuck after all.

I stepped back from the locker and stared at it for a minute. I had not worked there long, but I had hoped that maybe this time would be different. Seeing the locker empty like that gave me a weird feeling. You know people say it was like someone was walking over their grave? Sort of like that.

But I did not have time to dwell on that if I was going to make the shuttle. With a grunt, I shouldered the duffle bag. Then I tugged the front of my gray work coveralls to smooth them out and turned away. My work boots made hollow echoes as I walked out of the deserted room.

———

When I returned to my apartment three days later, I was exhausted. The kind of tired where you see spots and talk to someone only to realize you are totally alone. I barely had the energy and where-withal to kick my shoes off and drop my duffel before I collapsed onto my old threadbare couch.

Then I slept the sleep of the dead.

I came to eighteen hours later. It took a long moment to figure out where I was. I looked one way, then the other, and it was like I was staring at a foreign land.

Well, almost.

The pictures on the walls, the stuffed leather chair in the corner, the oversized video display unit on the wall, the kitchenette tucked into the rear corner, the door to the hall off to the left, a small door on the opposite wall leading into the bathroom, and behind me the double-doors that housed my pull-down bed were all familiar, but I could not place them at first. I was still that tired, even after that much sleep. Plus, I felt like hell; I had a sour taste in my mouth, like I'd been sucking on a lemon or something, and I ached all over.

Eventually it clicked. Home. A crappy little studio in a crappy portion of town.

No place like it.

It took a minute to push myself up off the couch. My aching muscles protested all the way. At least that made sense; I had worked hard on the station, though strangely my memories of what exactly I worked on were foggy. I chalked it up to my earlier exhaustion. Add to that the weird transition from full gravity to zero g on the shuttle to .5g on the station to zero g back to full gravity again and I was not the least bit surprised about the soreness.

I stumbled over to the little bathroom - it was the only separate room in my apartment - and, resting my hands on the sink, stared at myself in the mirror for a moment.

I *looked* like hell, too. Hair tussled, shadows under my bloodshot eyes. It was almost like I had been out drinking, except for the lack of headache.

"Get it together," I told myself, and pulled my toothbrush out of the medicine cabinet.

I was in the middle of brushing when I heard it. A rattling, or a scratching really, out in the main room.

More roaches? Sonofa... I just had the place fumigated a month ago. How could they be back so quickly? Muttering angry nothings under my breath, I dropped my toothbrush into the sink and stalked out into the room.

It was not roaches.

Whatever it was was shaking my duffle bag, almost as if something was inside and trying to get out. I gulped. I did not want to go see what this was. Killing bugs was one thing, but to make the duffle shake like that...was it a rat?

I used to play baseball in high school, then for a while in a local league. Though I don't play anymore, I kept my bat, a genuine Louisville Slugger. They are hard to find these days, and it was probably worth a bit of money, so it would have been a shame to get rid of it. Besides, I always told myself I would get back into baseball at some point; I used to be pretty good. In the meantime, the Slugger made for a handy home defense weapon from time to time.

I darted over and snatched up the Slugger from where it lay propped up against my stuffed chair. It made me feel a bit better to hold the solid wood in my hands. Rats ain't got nothing that can handle this.

Drawing a deep breath, I eased my way over to the still shaking duffle and, grabbing it by the zipper handle, dumped its contents.

The items from the bag tumbled out and I retreated a step, the Slugger held up, ready to swing. The clothes and towel landed in a heap, but the lunchbox rolled a foot or so before landing on its side. There was nothing else.

Ok...what was going on?

The lunchbox lurched and actually bounced a centimeter or so off the ground. I had to bite back a little yelp of surprise - not sure how well I succeeded - as I retreated another step and ran into the side of the couch.

The lunchbox lurched again. The rattling and scratching sound was louder now. The top of the box shook, and the latch holding it shut seemed to strain.

Inwardly, I willed the latch to hold. Whatever was in that lunchbox, I did *not* want it coming out. I should probably wail on it with the Slugger. I could probably bust the box up pretty good; that would at least knock silly whatever was inside it, give me time to figure out what to do with it. The food macerator under the sink drain sprang to mind, but I shoved that thought down. Too gross.

But I could not bring myself to move. I watched, Slugger held impotently at my side, as the top lurched and strained against the latch again. And again.

Then the latch broke and the lunchbox top flopped open, hitting the floor with a tiny metallic thud.

I gulped again.

Another rattle issued from the lunchbox and out crawled...a bunny rabbit?

———

What the hell was a bunny doing in my lunchbox? It was silly. Ludicrous.

But hang it all, it was darn cute.

A little white bunny, right out of an Easter Egg commercial. It hopped over toward me, its ears flopping in time with its hops in the most adorable manner. I'm no pansy, but I couldn't help it.

Nothing that cute could be bad. So I dropped the Slugger and squatted down.

It hopped over to me and I scooped it up in my arms. Its hair was smooth, soft, just the way you envision a bunny's should be. Its ears were perky, but flexible, and it had little white whiskers growing from its snout. Its eyes were pinkish-red; that made sense. The all-white coat meant it was probably an albino, the eyes just confirmed it.

The bunny snuggled in against my body and I pet it. It shivered, almost the way a cat will shiver when it purrs, and I could not help smiling. Questions of how it got into my lunchbox faded beneath the pleasure of cuddling it next to me. I sat down on the couch and activated the display. The bunny slid off my lap onto the cushion next to me, still vibrating soothingly.

The news was on. God, I hate the news. I glanced over at the timepiece on the wall. The game should be starting soon. Better to watch that than...

"Tragedy on Ketcham station," said the anchor, a severe-faced man in his early middle years who dressed like an undertaker, and I sat bolt upright, a chill going down my spine.

I could not have heard that right. I gestured for the display volume to increase, certain I was mistaken.

But I was not.

An image appeared on the display, clearly shot through a high-power lens, showing Ketcham Station's distinctive egg shape tumbling erratically through space. Gasses were streaming from several holes in the hull and the exterior navigation lights flickered on and off at random intervals, as though the circuitry or power supply had been compromised.

The anchor continued, his deep monotone speaking over the video. "Middle Earth Orbit Traffic Control lost contact with the station late last night after receiving a number of disturbing transmissions, followed by a distress call. While they struggled to regain contact, a nearby tug was vectored in and shot the video you are now watching. So far Traffic Control has been unable to link another craft with the station, and there is no word on the status of the two hundred and fifty scientists and support personnel who worked onboard. Family and friends of Ketcham Station employees can direct inquiries to..."

I slumped back against the couch, stunned, and let the rest of the anchor's words slide past without taking note of them. What the hell happened up there? I could not remember anything going seriously wrong. But then, I could not remember much of anything at all. I racked my brain, trying to think. There was the shuttle up, the young woman who greeted me at the airlock, and then...nothing. It was all a blur. Then something else sprang to mind, something that made the earlier chill in my spine turn into an icy feeling of dread.

How the hell did I get back home?

The bunny, still sitting next to me, squirmed. The little vibration it was making changed, becoming less soothing and more jarring, almost like when a musician hits the wrong note in a harmony part. I looked down at it, and dread turned into sheer terror.

———

This was no ordinary rabbit.

It crouched there on the sofa cushions, staring right back at me. Its irises, which before were albino pink, were now blood red, and its pupils were slits. Its ears were stiffer, their tips more pointed and also tinged with red. I became aware of something digging into my thigh through my pants and slid away. The thing's right front paw dropped down onto the cushion, leaving three little puncture wounds in my leg from long, sharp claws.

Run! Get up and run, jackass!

I felt like I was screaming that at myself, but I could not make my muscles respond. The best I could do was push as far away from it as I could, right up to the edge of the couch.

The thing just stared at me for a second. Then its lips drew back into a vicious little grin.

It had big, sharp, pointy teeth.

My muscles finally obeyed my mind's frantic pleas, and I bolted. I was off the couch in a heartbeat and heading toward the door. But the thing was faster. It snarled - a much louder snarl than I would have thought it capable of - and a second later it landed on my upper back, between my shoulder blades.

Pain flared from a dozen locations as the claws at the ends of its paws dug in. I thrashed around to try to get it off. Then a new, more intense pain came from the side of my neck.

I passed out.

———

I awoke to an awful pressure on my chest, as though a couple of burly guys were laying atop me. It was hard to draw breath. Very hard. As I slowly came around, I found myself wondering if my ribs would give way.

And then I opened my eyes.

I found myself staring straight into the bunny-thing's blood red gaze. I was lying on my back and it was sitting on my chest, staring at me. That's it. No big burly guys, just that little bunny-thing. It was a hell of a lot heavier than it looked. It noticed me waking up and grinned again. Its fangs were still there. More disturbing still, the fur around its mouth was stained red.

The ache in the side of my neck registered, and I flinched away as the source of the stains around the bunny's mouth became clear to me. Well, I tried to flinch, but the thing's weight prevented me from moving very far at all.

The thing's grin grew wider.

There's no point in trying to flee, Barry.

I heard the words in my head, but knew that the thought was not mine. Oh dear Lord it could read my...

Your blood is mine. I own you.

Its tongue caressed its fangs slowly, seductively. I had seen women use their tongues similarly, licking their lips while flirting. The display was quite a bit less arousing on this thing.

"What..." I cleared my throat, the tried again. "What are you?"

I am your master.

There was more than a hint of annoyance in the thought's tone. As though to accentuate its point, the thing dugs its fore-paws into my chest, sending lances of pain radiating from the area. I gritted my teeth, but groaned at the renewed discomfort.

"Stop."

Stop please, master.

It dug its claws in a bit deeper. It was as though someone was dripping molten metal onto my chest. For an instant, I had the notion of swiping it off of me. I was a strong guy; I should be able to do that. But the pain just escalated when I thought it. Worse, I found I could not move my limbs.

I had no choice. My ego rebelled against it, but I could not stand the pain any longer.

"Stop. Please." I had to draw a breath to get the last word out. "Master."

All at once, the pain ceased.

Good. The voice in my head sounded satisfied, pleased. *You learn quickly.*

I could not suppress a snort. *That* was something I had never been accused of before.

"What..." I cut off as the claws began digging in again, and the pain returned. I found myself groaning, and forced it down. Through gritted teeth I managed to mumble, "What do you want?"

The pain faded again, as quickly as it came. The bunny-thing looked at me for a long moment, its cat-like pupils narrowing in consideration. Another impulse to just shove it away came through me, but again it was as though my thoughts were disconnected from my body; I could not move a muscle.

Finally, it "spoke" again.

What I want... The creature's fangs seemed to lengthen, and I noticed little red stains on their tips. *I want food.*

I got a hollow feeling in my belly. Oh Lord, it was going to eat me.

It made a little coughing sound. Laughter?

You are not enough. Not for what I have to do. You will help me find more.

I somehow managed to swallow, despite having no saliva in my mouth. It could not mean what I thought it meant.

But it did.

————

I hugged my arms tight against my chest. Or as tightly as I could with the bunny - or whatever the hell it was - tucked into my trench coat with its nose poking out from the little V where the two flaps of the coat folded over each other.

I walked slowly down the street, a few blocks from my little apartment. The late autumn chill made my breath freeze in the night air in front of my face, but it was not the cold that made me shiver so.

It was the company.

The bunny monster had been insistent that we go out. I knew what it wanted, but I could not say no. Even when it was not digging its claws into me, I felt a...force...bearing down on my mind when it projected its desires into my head. I found myself doing its bidding before I realized what was going on.

I did not know how, but it had ahold of my mind. That was scary enough. The suspicion - no, the certainty - of what it sought was terrifying.

I went. Unwillingly, but I went trudging past the boarded up storefronts, the broken windows, the trash-laden streets. My little corner of Boston had never been the best neighborhood, but the last few years had been especially unkind. Businesses closed every week, or left for fairer shores despite the "best efforts" of the local officials to entice them to stay. I suppose all the promises of kick-backs and tax incentives in the world don't matter worth a damn if you can't enforce the basic rule of law.

Who would have figured?

My mind whirled as I picked my way past the detritus of a failing city, and I could not help but feel it was appropriate to bear the bunny monster with me down the dark streets. If any place would feel like home for it, this would.

Then I felt that pressure in my head again.

There.

I stopped abruptly, glancing around in confusion. What was it...

That one.

The thought came accompanied by pain as its claws dug into my chest. I grimaced to hold back a scream and stumbled forward, nearly bending over double. What was it talking about? Where...

Then I saw, and a new chill spread down my spine.

I knew. I knew without it having to tell me, but I did not want to believe the bunny monster really meant it.

But when the bunny monster's claws loosened their grip as I finally noticed the homeless man slumped against the wall of an alley ten meters ahead on the other side of the street and I felt that pressure in my mind again, I could not deny the truth.

We were out to get food.

I could not stop myself. My feet seemed to move of their own accord, jogging across the street in the wake of a passing Yellow Cab, then turning left toward the homeless man's alley. Against my chest, the bunny monster began purring, or whatever it was, again.

As we approached, I saw the man's features as clearly as if it were noon, and never mind that it was approaching midnight. Curly brown hair that hung in unwashed strands from his head. A matching beard, complete with bit of paper - or food? - caught in the long whiskers. High cheekbones and dark, defeated eyes. A ratty overcoat with several holes in it that he held close about his thin body, trying to preserve what little heat the thin garment would retain.

On any other night I might have thought about giving him a buck.

When I stopped in front of him and gestured into the alley, his eyes narrowed suspiciously. "Wha chu wan, buddy?"

Just as my feet had moved on their own, I found myself speaking before I realized what was happening. "Want to earn some money?"

The homeless man's eyebrow quirked upward, then he spat off to the side. "I don' turn tricks."

I felt the bunny monster's purring change, and I felt, faintly, a wry, almost derisive amusement seeping into my mind.

"No tricks. Job pays two hundred."

Both eyebrows climbed high on the man's forehead, and he suddenly grinned. He had several missing teeth and breath that would knock a moose over at twenty meters. It was all I could do not to gag. But then I found myself gesturing into the alley again.

This time the man nodded and, licking his lips, began walking in that direction.

As I followed him and the light from the street faded, it was like I was watching someone else. My heart pounded in my chest, and I could acutely feel every pulse through my my neck; the sound of my heartbeat was like a bass drum in my ears. My mouth grew dry and I found myself beginning to tremble. Was I really going to let this happen?

But I could not stop it.

The nameless man rounded a corner in the alley, taking us completely out of view from the street, and turned to face me. Before he completed the movement, the rabbit monster shoved itself off my chest and, springing from the low neck of my trench coat, landed on the man's chest.

He had enough time to voice a wordless shout of surprise, then the beast was on him. Its little head darted upwards, toward the side of his neck, and I heard as much as saw its fangs penetrate.

The man's eyes widened, and his shout became a rasping gurgle as he staggered backwards, his hands going reflexively to his neck, and the creature latched on there. He tugged at the bunny monster, but it did not budge. He stumbled back again, turning to the side as he did so, and slammed his back into the side of the building to my left. He beat on the bunny monster with his fists.

But it was all in vain. After maybe thirty seconds, he slumped to the ground. His eyes lost focus and rolled up in their sockets. His limbs began to spasm, his feet drumming against the alley's cement paving stones. Then, finally, he lay still.

I watched this happen, my feet glued in place. Though part of my brain shouted, "Run, you idiot!", another part was, unbelievably, fascinated.

I had never seen a man die before.

———

By the time we returned to my apartment, self-loathing consumed me.

What had I done? I let this...thing...kill that poor man. I did not even try to stop it. Worse, part of me had enjoyed it, or at least was not completely repulsed by it.

I slammed the door shut and flung my wallet and keycard onto the small table standing next to the door, then made quick work of removing my trench coat and hurling it into the corner. Then I stumbled over to the couch and collapsed. I pressed my palms against my forehead and felt myself on the edge of tears.

The bunny-monster, whatever it was, hopped slowly across the small room toward the couch from where it had landed when I took off the trench coat.

Rest. More tomorrow.

I found myself sobbing as I shook my head in denial. "No," I whispered. "I can't."

The pressure came crashing down on my mind again, and I felt its weight upon me as it hopped up onto my abdomen. Pain lanced through me as it landed and dug in.

Were its claws longer? It felt like it.

You will. You cannot stop me.

The pain grew greater, and I heard myself scream. Thankfully, I lost consciousness soon after that. But the monster's final words echoed through my mind as dreams took me.

———

It continued that way for the next week.

When I was not asleep, or engaged in biological necessities, the bunny monster rode me out onto the streets. And every time we went out, it took another victim. I lost track of the number of nameless schlubs the bunny monster killed, but it was a lot. And a slideshow of faces, all dead now, were emblazoned on my memory.

I saw them when I slept. I saw them in the bathroom mirror when I brushed my teeth and shaved. When the monster let me do those mundane things, anyway, which was not often. I could not escape the memory of those poor people.

At some point during the week, it struck me that I needed to go into work. Clark had not actually fired me, after all. He might not care, but presumably the company would care that I was alright, not dead on Ketcham Station.

And how exactly had that worked out, anyway?

I had no idea. I still could not remember what happened up there, though it was improving. Instead of essentially a big black blur of no memory at all, I slowly began to get flashes. Just individual images, an occasional face, a spoken word. Not enough to make any sense of. But it was something.

The point was moot, though. No sooner had I voiced the thought about returning to work than the bunny monster put the kibosh on it. I was not to go anywhere without it, and it was not going to my place of employment.

For a moment, before the pain began, I had the impression it was actually afraid of where I worked, for some reason.

Then I learned never to think on such things again.

———

By the end of the week, I began to notice a change. The bunny monster was larger.

But not all over.

Its claws had definitely grown - I had felt them too many times to not notice that. As had its fangs. The rest of its body, however, remained the same size it always had been.

Except for its belly.

At first I thought I was imagining things. It moved more slowly around my apartment, and when we went out and it pounced on a victim. But it was always a small enough difference that I could not be sure.

Then, one night, a week and a half after we first met, the bunny monster almost missed a meal. The poor schlub it picked out ducked its initial attack and ran away, screaming. For a moment, I thought he would actually get away, as difficult as the chase appeared to be for the monster. But finally, get him it did.

When it forced me back home, I looked at it - really looked - for a long time. There could be no doubt, now that I concentrated enough to really note the differences.

Its belly was most definitely larger. At one point, I swore I saw part of its belly move, even. I shrank back, swallowing hard. I thought I was past terror after the last week being held prisoner by that thing, but I felt a new, icy feeling of dread in my gut as I considered what I saw.

The bunny monster turned its head toward me right then. Its catlike eyes narrowed, seemed to grow more brightly red for a moment. Then it ran its little tongue over its lips and sniffed the air.

Soon.

The intruding thought echoed in my mind, its intensity making me rock back for a moment. The thought contained a deep, grim satisfaction, coupled with a primal eagerness that was barely contained. Were I that eager for something, I would be bouncing off the walls, but the bunny monster simply sat there, gazing at me with its unsettling eyes for a moment.

Then it smiled.

They will come soon.

That dread became sheer horror as I suddenly understood.

The creature was female.

How do you kill something that has complete, or near enough that it makes no difference, control over you? Something that you know from experience can kill *you* with little effort, and will if given the slightest cause to do so? Something that seems to know what you are thinking before you do?

That was the question that ate at my soul. Assuming I still had a soul, after what I had seen it do. What I had *allowed* it to do.

But I knew, sure as I was sitting there when the full meaning of the bunny monster's projected thought became clear to me, that this was what I had to do.

Under no circumstances could I allow that...thing...to give birth.

I could tell it sensed my revulsion as realization came over me. It's little lips turned upwards into a feral grin and it made a short, mocking, purring sound. Then it turned away and hopped over to its favorite side of my couch, where it nuzzled into the corner and went still.

The thing slept. It was a living creature, so of course it slept. Problem was, it usually slept when I did. On those few times when it had fallen asleep before me, it had been tempting to try something: to leave, to bash its brains in, something. Except that the very first time it slept in front of me, I did try something. Something so ridiculously minor it almost did not bear noticing.

Its rear paw was resting on one of my comic books. I tried to pull the comic out so I could read it. The bunny monster almost killed me.

Since then, I feared doing anything more than sitting or lying still. Even going to the bathroom in the middle of the night was a terror. I was tempted just to wet my bed and clean up later, except that I had no idea when later would be, since when the bunny monster was awake it allowed me to do nothing except bring it out for food or feed myself.

The apartment was beginning to stink bad enough without adding *that* sort of mess to it.

That afternoon, after the bunny monster's revelation, was the first time it had fallen asleep so early. Was it possible that I could find an opening somewhere?

I thought back over my life, back to when my mom was pregnant with my baby brother. I was ten, and I had no idea where my father was, but lo and behold here was a little brother, due for the world in a few months. When she told me, my feelings were mixed, but as time moved on I became more and more excited to have a brother, even one so much younger than I. That eagerness faded a bit when Mom grew - how do they put it? - "great with child". She was uncomfortable - hell, miserable - all the time. And she had only a fraction of the energy she normally did. I remember her sleeping a lot, and being damn hard to wake up.

It was that memory that convinced me I had a chance, even just a small one, to stop this thing before it got out of hand. And for some reason I was certain once that thing gave birth, that was exactly how things would become. Officially.

That just left figuring out how, exactly, to do it.

Seriously, how does one kill a vampire? I knew beyond a shadow of a doubt that was what the bunny monster was. Hell, I had seen it drink more blood than I ever thought possible.

I racked my brain, trying to recall all the little clues from vampire lore, but found nothing helpful.

More often than not, I cooked spaghetti for myself. It was quick and easy, and fit with the bunny monster's demanding schedule. I tried putting more than the usual amount of garlic in the sauce, hoping that the cloves would induce the bunny monster to leave. If anything, the smell of the garlic seemed to make it lick its lips with appetite.

Holy water? I did not have any, and I had no means to get any. But one night we walked past a church and I veered inside, just to see what would happen. The bunny monster's claws dug into me painfully, as expected, but no more or less than any other time I did not do exactly what it said. In fact, aside from its chagrin at my disobedience, it seemed perfectly comfortable within hallowed ground.

From that I deduced that holy blessings or other spiritual things mattered little to the bunny monster. And besides, in every story I could re-member you had to believe - really believe - in that stuff to make it work. That was not me.

So much for trying to ward it off with a crucifix.

What to do? Staring at it, its chest rising slowly with each inhalation as it slept, I just wanted to grab a butcher knife from the block in my kitch-enette and stab it to death.

But what if that didn't work? I shuddered to think of what it would do to me if I tried and failed. If it sucked me dry, like it did with those homeless men and women, would I live to feel the last drop leaving? Would part of me be trapped within it and its offspring, living - if you could call it that - in terror forever?

That was asinine, but I could not get the thought out of my head. So I sat there, impotent in my fear, and drifted off to sleep while I had the chance.

———

I awoke a short while later, sitting upright with a start. My heart was pounding, and I was wet with sweat.

The dream must have been a doozy, but I could not remember any of it. That was odd; I normally remembered most of my dreams. Going back over them helped ease the drudgery of my work days, a lot of the time.

Wiping the sweat off my brow, I decided it was probably just as well that I did not remember. Any dream that left me in such a state was best cast aside as quickly as possible. Besides, whatever the waking world, and the bunny monster, had to throw at me would be so much worse...

I glanced aside and did a double-take. The bunny monster was still asleep.

That was odd. Ever since it first arrived, it had awakened before I did. Most times, until the last couple days as its pregnancy grew more pro-nounced, it had been awake when I fell asleep as well. Oh, I had caught it napping a time or two, but rarely. This...this was unheard-of.

Moving carefully to avoid disturbing the bunny monster's cushion, I boosted myself up from the couch. As I reached my feet, I was struck by the urge to flee. Just run out the door and get the hell out of there. Go to the nearest police station and tell them what happened, so they could come in force and take the bunny monster down.

No sooner had I thought it than I recognized how stupid that thought was. The police would not believe me. Best case, they would ship me off to the funny farm. Worst case, they would lock me up and charge me with all those homeless people's deaths. Or both. By the time they realized I was telling the truth, the bunny monster would have given birth, and so, maybe, would have its offspring.

And then it would be too late.

No, there was no shoving the bunny monster problem off on someone else. I had to deal with it. And quickly.

But first, I needed to brush my teeth. They felt like they had a year's worth of accumulated gunk on them, but it had only been a week or so since I last managed the time to take care of that little chore, and I had a horrible metallic taste in my mouth.

I trudged over to the bathroom, scratching at an itch on my forearm, and tried hard not to notice how I smelled. I was sure I probably put those homeless people to shame.

I looked even worse.

The person brushing his teeth in the mirror was almost unrecognizable. Unkempt brown hair that was...going grey? When did *that* happen?...at the temples, a scraggly beard that also bore its share of silver, sunken eyes with dark half-circles below them. A stained green t-shirt with some obnoxious logo or other on the breast. All in all, I looked like hell boiled over.

I could not imagine why.

I swished and spit, and found myself transfixed by the sight of the water from the faucet as it took hold of the foamy residue from my mouth and swirled it down the drain.

I blinked, then spat again and watched it flow away. There was something about it...

An image flashed through my mind, like a single frame inserted into a movie, and I almost fell over. I had to grab the sides of the sink to keep my feet.

What the hell was that?

It came again, and I found myself sagging forward. My forehead touched the mirror, and I remembered.

I *saw*.

I was back on Ketcham Station, repairing some fried wiring in the rear of a backup lighting switchboard. They had experienced a minor malfunction that managed to knock out their primary lighting a couple days earlier. The backups had engaged automatically, of course. But several of the backup lighting strings failed, hence their urgent need for an electrician, once the initial malfunction was resolved.

The wiring in that particular switchboard was mostly intact, so I quickly finished, closed up the switchboard panel, and moved on. Or tried to move on.

The switchboard was directly opposite one of the station's research labs. What exactly they were doing was beyond me, and well above my pay grade, so I made sure not to pay too much attention. Easier to avoid trouble that way.

But something in the lab caught my eye, and I found myself stepping toward the large plexiglass window that separated the lab from the corridor where I was working. I glanced around, but none of the white lab coat wearing people noticed me. Their attention was fixed on some device toward the rear of the lab. I could not see what it was, but clearly it was important.

From another room, off to the left, a burly scientist entered the lab, carrying two wire mesh cages, one in each hand. Each cage held a cute white rabbit.

The bunnies seemed relaxed and content, even when the guy dropped their cages - quite abruptly - onto a countertop near the center of the room. Only when a couple of other researchers opened the cages, reached in, and yanked them out by the scruffs of their necks did the bunnies react, kicking and squirming in their captors' grips.

The researchers turned their backs to the window - to me - and carried the bunnies further back, toward the device I could not fully see, and I got a hollow feeling in the pit of my stomach. What were they doing to those little rabbits?

"What are you doing?"

The gruff female voice made me jump in surprise. I turned to see Dr. Liu, one of the more senior researchers on the station, glaring at me. She was in a white lab coat, like all the others, though her security badge had several more stripes of color than almost everyone else's did; she could go pretty much anywhere in the station she wanted. Her hair, still mostly black despite the fact that she was certainly in her mid fifties at least, was pulled back into a neat bun. All in all, she was not bad too look at...except for that glare.

I said something inane about just finishing up what I was doing and she grunted.

"Don't linger..." her eyes lowered and narrowed as she focused on my security badge, and my name, "...Barry. This is a security area. I'm sure there is more work for you elsewhere, yes?"

I nodded and, gathering up my tool kit, hurried away.

———

I blinked and came back to the present. Glancing out of the bathroom toward where the bunny monster lay waiting, I felt a surge of adrenalin flow. The image of the researchers manhandling those rabbits - they were so similar to the bunny monster - would not go away.

I shook myself to ward off the chill that was traveling up my spine. Whatever it was that was going on aboard Ketcham Station had no bearing on my problem: how to take down the bunny monster and free myself, while at the same time saving the Earth from an infestation of the buggers.

I pushed myself away from the bathroom sink and stepped back into the main room of my apartment. Again I looked over at the kitchenette, to the small block where I kept my cooking knives. Maybe it would work.

A rustling from the couch drew my gaze away, back to the bunny monster as it slowly stirred. It would be awake soon. Once it woke, I would have to put such thoughts out of my mind. I did not know how far the monster could go, whether it could just implant its own thoughts or read all of mine. But if it detected any hint of a plan to do it harm...

Things would get ugly, very quickly.

I hurried over to my corner of the couch and sat down, slumping back against the cushions as though I were still asleep. It would not do to have it wonder how long I had been awake, and what I had been doing. A small voice in the back of my mind whispered that it likely did not care, that it knew it had me cowed and was satisfied in its superiority. I forced that voice down, irritation mixed with disgust - at its sentiment as well as the fact that the sentiment was true - lending me extra strength to get my thoughts under control.

I waited.

At some point, I drifted back off to sleep. I did not realize it had happened until the bunny monster woke me with a pair of rough scratches along my forearm. That was how it always went in the morning; if I was not awake soon after it rose, I got a scratch. Never enough to draw blood, but enough to sting for a while and get me up.

It had never before had to scratch me twice.

I bolted awake, clutching at my arm and cursing softly, but the words died on my lips as I saw the bunny monster staring at me, its blood-red eyes narrowed into dangerous slits. If it were human, I would have said it wore accusation on its face.

Too much sleep.

I blinked; it also bore accusation in its thoughts. Had I given myself away somehow?

"Sorry. I..." I shook my head and rubbed at my eyes for a moment, then glanced at the clock. An hour had passed since I sat back down on the couch. It felt like five minutes. "I had an intense dream."

The bunny monster stared at me for another long moment, the turned and hopped off the couch, apparently satisfied.

Come. We hunt.

Obediently, I stood from the couch and went

to my coat rack to retrieve my jacket. As I prepared to go on another ghastly journey, I shifted
my thoughts back to the short nap I had taken. Intense dream. That was an understatement.

————

I was aboard Ketcham Station again. It was vivid,
every detail as plain and real as if I were actually
there.

I was taking a coffee break, sitting at a table in
the corner of the station's small cafeteria, and
nursing a steaming cup of what almost passed for a
decent brew. In that respect, it was a far sight
better than the coffee in most workplaces I had
been in since leaving the Navy. Just three scoops of
sugar and a couple dollops of cream was all it took
to make the coffee drinkable. That was one thing
about the Navy; those salty guys really do know
how to brew a mug. I tried to remind myself of all
the bad things, the reasons why I had gotten out.
But right then, sipping on that barely tolerable
mug of Joe, it was hard to remember.

I was not alone in the cafeteria, though I sat
alone at my table. A pair of men in researchers'
white lab coats stood on the other side of the
room, in front of the stainless steel of the service
station, and gave their orders. They would likely sit
together and leave me alone. One other table was
occupied, by a woman in workman's coveralls, but
she had her back to me and was watching the latest
ball game streaming on the live feed from
planetside.

So while I was not alone, I had my privacy,
which is the way I wanted it. Get in, do my thing,

and get out. That is how I preferred to do business, and this day was no different.

I turned my gaze away from the other in the room and stared down at my coffee, my thoughts drifting forward to rest of the morning's tasks. There was a faulty solenoid in the actuator on an emergency bulkhead seal door on deck three, a set of malfunctioning lights in the female berthing area on 01 level - that would be no fun; the hoops I would have to jump through just to get in there, let alone while I was in there working, saw to that - and a new fan to install in fan room six. It was a lot to do in one morning. But then again, the station was getting up there in years, and even without the recent malfunctions there was plenty to do to keep up the aging infrastructure.

"...very promising results."

Nearby voices drew my eyes from my mug. The two research men were settling down into plain white plastic chairs at the table next to me. They each held a bagel on a small plate in one hand and a cup in the other. Their security badges were only slightly less striped than Dr. Liu's had been. That meant they were high in the chain, though I did not recognize them. Which was hardly surprising since I had just reported aboard.

The research man who spoke wore a large grin on his face. His companion was less cheerful.

"How can you say that?"

"It almost worked, and the data we got will help us refine the settings. Next time..."

The glum researcher waved off his colleague's comments. "Data, shmata. Did you see what happened to that rabbit? The portal..."

He stopped talking, seeming to notice me for

the first time. His mouth shut with an audible clack of teeth striking teeth and he scowled.

"This does not concern you," he said, looking right at me. His tone became cold, biting. As the man spoke, his cheerful companion followed his gaze with a stare of his own. His lips, turned upward a moment ago, compressed into a scowl.

I recognized what that meant. Part of me wanted to protest that I was here first and they were intruding on my private time. But I knew that would do no good and likely land me in trouble besides, so I stood up. "Sorry, gents. I was just leaving."

I slipped around their table, trying not to feel my head being ripped apart beneath the weight and economy of their combined stares. The coffee sucked anyway. I walked over to the trash can near the doorway and tossed it, plastic mug and all. Then I took a minute to sling my tool bag over my shoulder. Before I left, I heard the researchers begin speaking again, more quietly this time but still loud enough to easily carry to where I was standing.

"...Just a few setting changes and the quantum tunneler will be operational. And when that happens, who cares what happened to a couple of stupid rabbits..."

That was the cheerful one again. His voice cut off abruptly as the door slid shut before me. I was happy to hear it go; I had work to do.

———

The Quantum Tunneler.

The bunny and I were walking the streets

again, looking for the bunny monster's next victim. I hardly noticed where it was taking me, the people around me, or the time of day. Which was unusual; it - she - had almost never taken me out during the day, let alone on a hunt at that time. And yet there we were. She must really be hungry to throw caution to the wind like this. But I did not care. Maybe I should have, but I did not. My mind kept going back to those words.

The Quantum Tunneler. That was important, and I could have sworn I had heard those words before. But from where?

That one.

The bunny monster's insistent thoughts intruded rudely into my head, forcing me out of my contemplation as it directed me to the right, toward a woman sitting alone on a bench a half block down the street from where I stood.

I hated when the bunny monster took women.

As we approached, I saw that the woman was not like the other victims had been. She was young, with red-gold hair and a lovely face. Her clothing and jacket were inexpensive but not in disrepair. There was no odor of alcohol around her, and she did not seem beaten down by the world. Rather, she appeared cheerful. Not at all like the others.

She saw me coming and quirked an eyebrow upward. "Spare some change, mister? I'm on the road," she said. Her voice was clear, strong. Optimistic.

I shook my head, a negative meant for the bunny monster, not for her.

Not her; the monster could not have her. I tried to veer away, but I felt the claws dig in deep.

Deeper than usual; deeper than they ever had after that first day with the monster. I had to bite my lips to keep from crying out from the sudden agony.

"Mister?" The girl sounded concerned. "You ok?"

I curled my arms over my chest and tried again to turn away. Maybe I could keep the monster form reaching her...

But, despite its increased bulk, the bunny monster remained more than limber. It squirmed against my chest, digging its claws in with each move, and forced itself out of the V in my trench coat. There it paused for the briefest of moments, casting a baleful look at me that promised pain and worse.

The girl saw it. Her concern became confusion, followed by enchantment. "What a cute bunny..." He words were lost in a shriek of sudden terror as the bunny monster bared its fangs and leapt at her.

It should have got her. Should have killed her and feasted on her blood, just as it had so many others. But somehow, in that one moment, I was the faster. As it leapt, I lunged forward, stretching my arms like a wide receiver going for a pass that was just slightly overthrown, but never actually expecting to catch the thing. When I felt soft fur in my hands, I almost let go in surprise and shock. Hell, the bunny monster froze in shock as well; or at least I presume it was in shock. Regardless, it did not move in those couple seconds I had it in my grasp.

I did not stop to wonder at the turn of events. Instead, I turned and hurled the bunny monster away, as hard as I could. It flew through the air, tumbling head over fluffy tail in a way that, in different circumstances, would actually have been funny. Then it struck an overturned trash can at the entrance of a nearby alley.

Part of me wondered, hoped, that the impact had killed it, but I knew better. At most it would delay the bunny monster's attack, only now it would come after me as well as the girl. We had to get out of there, and fast.

I turned back to her. She was looking at me with wide, fearful, but confused eyes and her mouth was agape.

"What... What..." she stammered.

But this was no time for explanations. "Run!" I cried, and shoved the back of her shoulder, turning her around and propelling her away from the bunny monster's landing spot before she could raise a word of protest.

Amazingly enough, she ran. I could not understand it at first. Maybe it was because the whole situation was just too weird. Maybe I managed to put enough fear and command in my tone that she decided it would be better to do what I said, at least for the moment.

Or maybe it was the roar - an actual honest to God roar - of fury that the bunny monster made before it set out after us.

I had seen how quickly it could move. Its small body was deceptive, and I knew it could catch us easily if we did not get out of there, and fast. Problem was, get out of there to...where? All up and down the street, shops were boarded up. The few that were not were open for business, their entrances standing wide open to admit customers.

Not exactly an ideal place to run, where the bunny monster could easily follow.

There were cars, though. A steady stream of cars flowed down the street, and every so often a cab. If I could flag one of them down, we could... I shelved the thought as soon as it reared its head. In the time it took to get a cab, the bunny monster would be on us. And besides, I had no money on me and I doubted the girl did either. She *had* just been begging for spare change.

"What is that thing?" the girl asked in between gasps. She was getting winded quickly, a bad sign.

"Long story," I said, knowing it was a lame answer. I cast around, looking for something, anything, and then I saw it. At the corner of the next block, across the street: a T station. If we could get down there and onto a train... "Come on," I said, and picked up the pace. I was already running at well beyond a comfortable pace, but now that I had a goal in sight, there seemed no point in holding back.

The girl opened her mouth, to protest I thought, but just then the bunny monster roared again and I heard a crash from astern. Looking back over my shoulder, I saw that it was rapidly closing the distance; it was maybe twenty yards behind us now. The crash was from another garbage can. The bunny monster must have knocked into it, because it lay on the ground in the monster's wake, rolling away slowly as it spilled its contest onto the sidewalk.

Gross.

But it spurred the girl on to greater speed.

We charged down the street. I heard the bunny monster behind us, but I did not dare look back again. It would cost too much speed. The T-station was only a short distance ahead, and I began to think we might make it.

Then something solid and sharp struck me in the center of my back and I stumbled forward, landing face-first on the sidewalk.

It had me. I could hear its breathing, feel its claws digging in as it scurried up my back toward my neck. Briefly, I thought it would just punish me and that would be it; everything could go back to the way it was. Or maybe I hoped that. But deeper down, I knew that was not the case. It meant to drink me dry, then have the girl as well. After all, it did not really need me anymore; it had had its nourishment and was about ready to deliver its babies. Whether it killed me now or in a day or two was immaterial at this point.

I squirmed, trying to roll over and slam my weight into it, but again the bunny monster seemed to weigh more - much more - that it should have. And when it thumped down on my shoulder blades with its front paws, I found myself slammed into the sidewalk again.

Fool.

Its thought entered my mind, and with it images. Horrible images. The things it planned to do to the girl after it finished me. And then to others once its babies were born. I had always known it would be bad, but to *see* it... I screamed then, and not just because I feared for myself.

But then, suddenly, I heard an impact above me, felt a lurch, and the bunny monster was gone.

I looked up in time to see the girl following through on a kick. The bunny monster's excessive weight must have been a trick of the mind, because it sailed through the air and landing hard in the street. Right in the path of a delivery truck.

The driver tried to hit the brakes, but the bunny monster landed too close. The squeal of skidding tires and the smell of burning rubber reached us at the same moment as the, softer, sound of the bunny monster going SQUISH beneath the truck's left front tire.

I rolled over and pushed myself up onto my elbows, ignoring the pain in my back and chest for the moment as I stared at the truck's tire. I could see one of the bunny-monster's rear legs sticking out from under it, unmoving.

My mind screamed out in protest. Seriously? It could not be that easy. I had lived in terror and guilt for how long, fearing to lift a finger to that thing and letting it do all the things it had done, and in the end it was *that* easy to kill? All at once, my disbelief turned into guilt, and disgust at myself. I had been such a coward.

I flopped back onto the sidewalk - the new wounds in my back screamed in protest, but I ignored them - and pressed the palms of my hands to my eyes, trying to ward back tears of remorse and pain.

The girl's voice interrupted my self-pity party. "You ok?"

I lowered my hands and found myself looking up at her face, which was only a foot or two above mine; she was crouching down next to me. "Been better," I said softly.

She looked me up and down quickly, then nodded agreement. "Hope so." Gee thanks, lady. "What was that thing?"

I groaned and forced myself into a seated position. "You wouldn't believe me if I told you."

She snorted. "Try me."

Just then I heard a creaking, from over by the delivery truck. I turned my head, and saw the impossible.

The truck's tire was moving, bulging out in places and then returning to normal, as though something was squirming around beneath - or within - it, trying to get out.

"Oh no," I said as cold dread filled me. I began pushing myself to my feet. "We gotta get out of here."

"What?" asked the girl. "Why?"

I found my feet and pointed at the tire. Her eyes widened in renewed fear.

The bunny monster was still alive.

A small crowd had gathered, people dressed in everything from dirty clothing little more than rags to tailor-made suits. They clustered around on the sidewalks, staring at us, at the truck, but most of all at the tire as it squirmed around. They were all in danger from that thing, but I couldn't worry about that. The bunny monster's first desire would be to get me. And the girl, whoever she was. It wanted her, above and beyond the others - there were surely many others - that we had passed on the street that morning.

I grabbed at her arm, half expecting her to push me away when my fingers closed. But for wonder, she did not, transfixed as she was by the sight of the bunny monster struggling to free itself.

"We have to get out of here," I said as fiercely as I could while still keeping my voice low, so it would not carry.

She was trembling intensely. Her eyes were fixed into a terrified stare, and she did not respond.

I snapped my fingers in front of her face and she jerked.

"We have to go. Now!"

She nodded quickly, in fearful jerks.

That was enough for me. I grabbed her arm more firmly and pulled her along behind me as I made a beeline for the T station, now only a few tens of meters away.

———

The train door slid closed and we slumped down onto the plastic seats, drained. A few seconds later, the train began moving down the track in the direction of Alewife. Not that I intended for us to go that far. Downtown Crossing was just a few stops ahead; we could get off there with all sorts of options while I figured out what to do next.

As the train's acceleration picked up, the girl shook herself as though rousing from a daydream. And perhaps she thought she was; all power to her if she found that comforting.

The look on her face said she did not.

"Alright, what the hell *was* that?" she asked, her voice still trembling.

I shook my head. "You wouldn't believe me."

"You said that before. Tell me."

I looked at her for a moment. She was obviously shaken, afraid, but she was gathering herself quickly. More quickly than I had, the first time I met the bunny monster. In fact, she looked... I blinked. I had not really noticed before how good she looked. I mean, I had noticed, but not *noticed*. And really, she was a looker.

I suddenly became aware of how God-awful I probably looked, in clothes that had not been washed in who knows how long, to say nothing of how I probably smelled. I looked away, feeling the heat of an embarrassed blush creeping onto my cheeks.

I heard her sigh, in exasperation I thought. I was going to lose her in a second. So, I spilled it.

All of it.

From getting "transferred" to Ketcham Station, to winding up at my apartment, to the bunny dominating me for all this time. I told her all of it, and it was like a weight had been lifted. Just to tell someone else what the hell was going on felt good, comforting. The fact that no one else was sitting anywhere near us did not hurt. She, at least, stood a chance of believing me, after what she had seen.

I finished and she responded with only silence.

I looked back at her and saw that she was chewing on her lip thoughtfully. She still did not say anything.

"Well?" I asked, when I could bear the silence no more.

"You were really on Ketcham Station? I heard there were no survivors."

I blinked. I had never seen any news updates about the station's status, but then I had been a bit distracted. I suppose I had just assumed they rescued everyone. To hear differently was...

Wait a minute.

"No survivors? None?"

She shook her head.

"Holy Cannoli," I breathed. Now *that* was

something I had not considered. Hell, for all I knew, they probably had me listed as deceased, since I had no idea if I checked in with anyone when I left the station or arrived planetside. Hell, I *still* did not know how I managed that at all.

If I was officially dead, that opened up whole realms of possibilities. For later.

The girl looked at me with a quizzical expression. "So you think this thing came back with you from the station." It did not sound like a question, but the way her eyebrows rose as she said it spoke volumes about how much she doubted I was correct. Or telling the truth. Or something.

I nodded, spreading my hands helplessly.

"So what the hell *is* it? Cause it sure ain't a bunny rabbit."

I shook my head. "I really don't know." My thoughts flashed back to the dream from the previous night, and the things I remembered yesterday. "I... I think they were doing some kind of experiments up on the station. They had rabbits...and a device of some sort. I think whatever they were doing went wrong and..." I made a vague gesture toward the rear of the train. "Now it's like it's a vampire or something. At least that's how it acts. All I know for certain is it's going to have babies soon, and once that happens..." I left the rest unsaid.

The girl nodded slowly. "So what, it wanted to eat me next?"

I nodded. She was remarkable calm about that part.

"Why didn't you let it?"

"What?"

"You let it eat the others. Why not me?"

"I... I didn't *let* it! I..."

She just stared at me levelly until I dropped my eyes to the floor, all the guilt and shame I had felt the last several days welling up again. She was right, of course. I stopped it from getting her; I could have stopped it with any of them. Or figured a way to kill it. Something. Anything, besides being a passive vessel for that damned thing.

Everything that had happened was my fault

I felt tears - of shame, of guilt, of accumulated stress - welling up, but I refused to let myself cry. Instead, I sniffed and wiped them away, and forced myself to look back at her.

She had asked a legitimate question. But how to explain that she alone of the bunny monster's chosen victims was not one of the dregs of society? That she was, well, pretty. Too pretty for me to allow her to come to that end. Just thinking it made me cringe at how shallow a reason it was.

Instead, I just shrugged. "I'd had enough of it." That much was true, at least.

She nodded slightly. "Fair enough." Her tone said she suspected there was something more, but thankfully she did not press. "Well." The next station was coming up; she stood and held out her hand to me. "Thank you, I suppose."

Surprised, I took her hand. She gave mine a quick shake, then turned toward the train door.

"What are you doing?"

She looked back at me, confused. "I'm getting off this train and then I'm calling the cops."

"Uh...miss, I don't think..."

The train came to a stop and the door opened. The girl turned her back on me and stepped down the stairs and off the train.

Something small and white jumped off the top of the train and crashed onto her back, and she went down.

It had followed us.

———

I stood transfixed for a second. In shock. In disbelief. In horror. How? *How* had it followed us, staked out the very car we were riding in? Not that I should have been surprised at all; the thing was nothing if not relentless and effective when it set itself to a goal. That much had become abundantly clear in the time it kept me prisoner.

But...damn...

The sound of the girl's scream broke me out of my reverie, and I bounded forward. The chimes that announced the doors would be closing sounded, and I threw myself out of the train. If I did not make it out of the train to help her, she was done. I knew that without question.

I felt the door tug at the sole of my shoe, and for a moment I wondered if my foot was caught and I was about to be dragged along beside the train car. But then the pressure on my shoe eased as my momentum carried me forward. I landed sprawling on the concrete of the station's floor at the same time as I heard the solid thud of rubber striking rubber, signaling that the door had seated.

Then the train pulled away.

I pushed myself onto my feet and moved toward the girl. She was squirming and flailing about with her arms and legs, trying to dislodge the bunny monster, but it held fast. And was steadily making its way up her back to her neck.

I glanced around, hoping another commuter or two would be able to help, but the station was empty. How was that possible, at this hour of the day? But it was, and all the wishing in the world was not going to change that. It was, again, all up to me.

A good solid kick had dislodged the thing from my back. I charged froward, hoping the same would work here.

But the bunny monster was waiting.

Maybe it expected my move. Or maybe attacking the girl was just a ruse meant to make me show myself, so it could exact some revenge. For whatever reason, it was ready. When I drew back to kick, it launched itself toward me. As it flew toward my face, I could clearly see its eyes, bright red to reflect its anger and blood lust, the pupils narrowed to tiny slits as it put all its attention on me.

I was moving forward with too much momentum. I could not just stop, or hop backwards. In the split second before the bunny monster struck me, I considered doing both and just as quickly dismissed them. In the end, I did the only thing that seemed reasonable: I raised my forearms in front of my face and dropped to the ground, fully expecting to feel the bunny monster's claws digging into my arms, followed by its fangs on my throat.

But that did not happen.

Somehow, my dive made it miss.

Unbelieving, I rolled onto my back and sat up. Beside me, the girl had done the same, but unlike me she did not stop there, but was beginning to stagger to her feet.

The bunny monster lay at the base of a concrete pillar a few meters away. For a second, I thought perhaps it had sailed into the pillar and crushed its head. No such luck. It turned to face us - to face *me* - and stared for what felt like forever. Then it growled. No, roared.

"Oh my God," the girl breathed, scampering to her feet.

I was forced to agree. I wracked my brain, trying to think of something, anything I could do. But how do you kill a vampire?

"What?"

I had not realized I had spoken the thought out loud. I gestured toward the bunny monster. I had begun to advance, slowly for now as though savoring the moment of our fear. "How do you kill a vampire?"

I began backing away from the thing, toward the stairs leading up to the street level. The girl did the same, never taking her eyes off the bunny monster. "I don't know...holy water? Garlic?"

I was about to tell her that was not going to work, and we did not have those things anyway, but the bunny monster picked that moment to charge.

Predictably, it went for the girl first. Was it *trying* to piss me off, or did it really think I had so little thought in my head that it assumed I would act stupidly again just because she was in danger? More than likely the later. And, in its defense, I *did* do something stupid because she was in danger.

I leapt in front of her, shielding her with my own body.

———

If I had taken a minute to think about it, there is no way I would have put myself in the bunny monster's line of fire. A loud voice in the back of my head screamed, "What the hell are you doing?", but it was far too late to pay any heed to the voice of reason. The thing was coming right at me now, and I only had time to react by instinct. I barely had time to get my hands up before the bunny monster struck me.

But somehow, that was enough.

I stood there, stunned, and looked at the diminutive beast that I had somehow caught in midair before it would have landed on my throat. I held it beneath its front legs, and could feel the bones of its ribs quite plainly beneath my fingers.

For a second, we just looked at each other. I think it was as surprised at my miraculous catch as I was, if the widening of its eyes was any indication.

Then the second passed and it opened its mouth wide, barring its fangs. It began squirming around in my grip, trying to break free. It was all I could do to keep my hands locked around it, but I managed. Then it began scratching at me. Its forelegs clamped onto the muscles of my forearms, and the claws dug in. Deep. Far deeper than it had scratched at me before, even the first time when it was asserting its dominance. No, these blows were intended not to subdue but to punish, and punish severely.

And boy did they do the trick.

Searing pain, beyond anything I had ever felt, ran up my arms, and I saw red. I heard myself crying out - hell, screaming - but was not conscious of actively doing so. The world compressed until it consisted only of the pain and the image of the bunny monster's eyes, glowing as though lit by a red fire. That was all I could see.

Kneel.

The command crashed into my mind like a sledgehammer. I only *thought* the bunny monster had been forceful before. This... This was like nothing I had ever experienced or dreamt of. I was down on my knees in an instant; it was like the bunny monster had directly controlled my leg muscles to get me there.

The pain lessened slightly, enough that I could make out more than just the bunny monster's eyes: its entire face came into focus, now just inches away from mine. How I managed to not lose my grip on it completely, I had no idea, but somewhere beneath the pain and the pressure on my mind I felt the soft fur of its coat.

Release me.

This order was less like a sledgehammer and more like a soothing caress. It contained promises of an end to pain, of comfort even. It was like an offer of lemonade on a humid summer day while lying in a hammock with a gentle breeze blowing past you. I wanted to give in, and not because of the pain of my newest wounds, but because of that promised bliss.

I knew it was a lie, but all the same I felt my fingers beginning to relax. It wouldn't be so bad to just let go, let it all go.

No!

Somehow, I thought of all the people it had taken - had forced me to help it take. Of the vile babies growing in its belly. Of the havoc those babies would cause. And I became angry. Furious.

That anger beat back against the pressure of its mental command, and I felt myself regaining control.

"No" I growled, and I began squeezing, as hard as I could.

The bunny monster's eyes grew wide, whether in surprise or anger I was not sure. But a moment later, as I felt its ribs beginning to give beneath the pressure of my hands, I knew the expression taking shape on its face was pain. And, I knew for certain, fear.

I felt more than a little satisfaction from that.

The beast began squirming madly. Its foreleg claws, already dug into my arm, began pulling downward toward my hands, and I saw deep ruts begin to open in my flesh. Its rear legs kicked up and I felt a new pain as those claws struck the undersides of my upper arms and held fast.

I was not going to win this contest. Either I would lose my grip from pain, or shock, or blood loss. But sooner or later I would let go, and then it would be all over.

Fortunately, I was not fighting alone.

From out of nowhere, or at least that was how it seemed to me, something crashed down onto the bunny monster's head. I heard the hollow clank of metal striking bone and, all at once, the bunny monster went limp.

It also dropped out of my grasp, unprepared as I was for the sudden additional force.

I stumbled backwards, reeling and for a second unable to comprehend what had happened. Then finally my vision cleared and I saw the girl crouching over the bunny monster, a fire extinguisher held in both of her hands.

She brought the base of the extinguisher down on the beast's head over and over again. There was a crack, then a squishing sound, and then its head broke open completely and grey matter splattered out all over the concrete floor. Only then did she stop. She pushed herself to her feet, dropping the extinguisher to the ground, and stumbled backwards until her back struck another pillar.

The only sound for a long several seconds was that of the extinguisher rolling away from where she had dropped it.

"Good Lord," I breathed. I wanted to say something - several somethings - more colorful. The burning in my arms alone seemed to call for it. But for some reason, just then I felt like swearing would have been wrong, sacrilegious almost.

The girl just stared at the bunny monster for a few seconds more. Then she looked back at me. Her eyes were haunted, but that quickly changed when she saw me. Or more in particular, when she saw the vast amounts of blood leaking from my forearms.

"Oh God," she cried, and hurried over to my side. "Are you alright? Put pressure on it."

Like I didn't know that. I somehow managed a half-smile. "I don't know. Hope so." I drew a deep breath and held it for a second, focusing only on that action. It seemed to help with the pain. A very little bit. "Thanks," I added.

She nodded, but only briefly. She took my hands and raised them so she could examine the wounds in my forearms more closely. "You're going to need stitches, quickly, or you're going to be in trouble." She turned her head side to side, scanning the station quickly. For what, I was not sure until she spoke again. "We need to put on a bandages. Can you get out of that coat?"

Despite the pain, I managed a resigned chuckle. My trench coat was totally destroyed. Between the scratches the bunny monster had put in the back and now the sleeves... The thing hung in tatters. All the same, it took some doing, and no small amount of assistance from her, to get it off.

She saw the t-shirt I was wearing and rolled her eyes, but said only, "That cotton will be a better dressing. Take that off, too."

That was quite a bit more difficult and painful to do, but I managed. Once the t-shirt was off, she began tearing it into strips using a small pocket knife she pulled from seemingly out of nowhere. It took me far too long to realize she kept it - duh! - in her pocket. I was losing a lot of blood.

Very quickly, she had what she needed, and she began dressing my wounds. She was very precise and neat in how she tied off the dressings, as though she had a lot of practice doing this sort of thing.

I cleared my throat. "Do this a lot?"

She blinked, pausing what she was doing, then flushed slightly. "I studied nursing for a while," she said. She went back to work. A few minutes later, my forearms looked like those of a mummy, but at least I was not dripping blood everywhere. "That should keep you until you can make it to a hospital."

"Thanks," I said, trying another smile. It was easier this time; the pain had reduced quite a lot, the way it tends to in the aftermath of wounds. A thought hit me. "You know, I never got your name."

The girl stared at me for a second. She looked surprised, then she just shook her head and laughed. "Sheila," she said, and we shook hands again. More gently this time.

"Barry."

"Nice to meet you, Barry."

"You too. I..."

I glanced past her shoulder toward where the bunny monster's body lay, and my words caught in my throat.

It was gone.

"Oh crap," Sheila breathed when she saw it. "Where the hell is it?"

I shook my head, unable to fully comprehend what I was seeing. How could it have gotten back up from that? It's brains were splattered all over the floor. Hell, some of them were still splattered all over the floor. So what the hell?

"Barry, what do we do?" She sounded well past freaked out. So was I, for that matter.

I drew in a deep breath and picked up what was left of my trench coat. My t-shirt was gone, so it was wear that or walk around topless, and it was getting a bit chilly for that. "We get the hell out of here," I said as I straightened.

Sheila nodded, her eyes darting back and forth in a fearful scan of the area.

She took my hand as we turned toward the stairs. Not from any romantic impulse, I was sure. But it still felt nice. I gave her hand a little squeeze and started up the stairs.

It was not until we reached the top that I realized how screwed we were.

———

"Are you freaking kidding me?" Sheila was well past scared and more than a little frustrated, and it showed in her strident tone as she shouted the words.

I could not blame her.

At the top of the stairs, the retractable steel bars that closed off the station after the T shut down for the night were closed and locked with a padlock that appeared nigh-on indestructible. I checked the time on my watch - somehow it still functioned. 2:30 pm. What the hell??

That explained why no one else was in the station. But why was it shut up? And why would the train stop at a station that was closed?

I shook the bars, knowing it to be futile even as I tried it. But that's what you do when you encounter a barrier in your way: at least try to see if there is an easy way to get past it.

"Oh crap, Barry. What are we going to do?"

That was the second time in as many minutes that Sheila asked that question, and this time I had no answer. The thought of going back down there, where the bunny monster waited, somewhere, was unacceptable. But waiting up here, where there was no where to go, was not much better.

I looked out, past the bars, at the street outside. The station was set ten or fifteen meters back, but I could see a number of pedestrians walking along the street. This area of town was much better than the one we had left not so long ago. If we could get one of those pedestrians to call for help, we might be able to...

Then it hit me how stupid I was being.

"You have a mobile? Mine's sitting on the coffee table at home."

Sheila blinked, then her eyes lit up. She fished in the inner pocket of the light jacket she wore, then pulled out her phone with a smile of triumph. She punched in 911 and held the device up to her ear. She bounced from foot to foot eagerly as she waited; she was practically dancing, the way she was going on.

A few seconds later, her eyes widened, and she said, "Yes. Hello? Look my friend and I need help."

She continued speaking with the operator, but I put the conversation out of my mind. Now that she was engaged, I went down a few steps and peered down into the station. The bunny monster was down there. It was certainly injured, and pissed off to no end as well - that was probably putting it mildly. And it would not be hard to figure out where we had gone. Fortunately, we ought to be able to see it coming from here.

Sheila hung up the phone and came down to stand beside me. "They'll be here in about fifteen minutes, with someone from the transportation department who can let us out." She did not sound particularly pleased. For that matter, neither was I.

"What did you tell them?"

She frowned, looking sidelong at me. "That we are locked in here and had been attacked by an animal."

I snorted softly. Attacked by an animal. While true, it was rich. "Well I guess we wait then."

Sheila nodded. She glanced down the stairs and I could see she was still more than nervous. She licked her lips. Her momentary elation at talking to the authorities was wearing off fast. I needed to get her mind off things, keep her calm.

I needed to do the same thing for myself.

"Why did you stop nursing school?"

Sheila gave a little start, then made a little sound that was half sob, half chuckle. "Ran out of money," she said, her eyes never leaving the landing, some thirty steps below us.

"There are scholarships..."

Sheila snorted. "Not for me. Just drop it, ok?"

I raised my hands defensively. "Ok. Sorry."

We sat in silence for a while. Or at least it felt like a while before Sheila spoke again.

"Do you think it's..."

"Dead?"

She nodded.

I shook my head. "Getting run over by a truck didn't kill it. I doubt a fire extinguisher will do the trick."

Frowning, Sheila looked back down the stairs toward the empty station below. I followed her gaze, not wanting to say what I knew to be true: that as soon as it got over the shock of being whacked on the head a few times, the bunny monster would be coming for us.

We didn't have fifteen minutes.

I crept back down the stairs slowly, easing each foot down onto the stair below before shifting my weight onto it to avoid making noise. It would have felt a bit comic - hell, I had to suppress the feeling that I looked a fool - but rising fear stamped down my self consciousness in favor of flight-or-fight.

I glanced over my shoulder to where Sheila sat, her back pressed up against the metal bars that sealed the entrance to the station. She managed a quick smile and thumbs up. Brave girl. She was clearly terrified, but was trying not to show it. I wondered how well I was doing in that regard.

Then I lowered myself down into the station proper, and I stopped, listening and looking.

The spot where the monster attacked me, and where Sheila knocked it for a loop, was easy to see from the smear on the floor. But aside from that, there was no visible indication of where it might have gone. The only noises were the soft hum of the fluorescent lights that illuminated the station and of ventilation fans whirring softly away in their ducts. Of course, the whole place smelled like crap.

It was not going to be easy to find this thing.

Listening to the fans, I considered briefly whether the bunny monster had crawled into the ventilation ducts and from there up to the surface, but quickly discarded the thought. It was not as nimble as it had been when we first "met", and the babies were clearly coming any time. Chasing Sheila and I, hitching a ride on the T, and surviving the truck and Sheila's attack must have drained a good portion of its energy. I let myself hope that it had crawled away into a corner to sleep, and maybe I could dispatch it while it was unconscious.

Fat chance.

I walked slowly across the wide open area past the entrance turnstiles, looking back and forth for any other sign of the monster, and saw nothing. Not a thing. There was not even a smear or streak leading away from where it had fallen. I continued on and found I had to force myself to breathe regularly. My heart pounded in my ears and it seemed like every step I took echoed loudly throughout the station, no matter how carefully I set my feet.

And so I was surprised to hear a rustling sound. Faint, almost inaudible, but it was there, off to my right, behind a closed-up concessions cart.

I thought for a second that it was just a rat, but I knew that was just wishful thinking. Part of me - a huge part - screamed to run, just get away from the thing. But the small little window of reason that I had been working so hard to maintain recognized that would be futile. The bunny monster had already proven more than willing and able to track me me down, and probably Sheila now as well, even on a moving train. Surely it would catch me on foot without any trouble at all.

And besides, where was I going to go? Down the train tracks into the darkness of the tunnels in between stations, where a train would likely run me down without noticing?

I froze in mid-step, not even realizing I had begun walking toward the concession cart, as the details of that idea struck me. Those tunnels all had maintenance accesses, walkways, things like that. Maybe we *could* get away through them, down to the next station. It could not be more than a quarter mile at most; that would just take a few minutes, and then we could get out.

Almost on cue, a low rumbling began to emanate from the tunnel leading off to the south, where we had come from. It got slowly louder, and I felt my heart leap. Another train! Maybe I could flag it down, and we would not have to walk, even.

I turned and dashed back to the turnstiles at the bottom of the stairs and gestured frantically for Sheila to come back down. She blinked, looking confused, then unbelieving. She shook her head, lips turned downward in a deep, frightened frown.

The rumbling was even louder, and I could see the light from the approaching train's headlights begin to brighten the tunnel's curve where the track bent out of sight to the south. Damnit, we were going to miss our chance!

I gestured again, more forcefully, and pointed toward the track. She could not see it, not from where she stood. I silently prayed - it had been ages since I'd done that with any regularity - that she would get my gist and move it.

The rumbling of the train grew louder. Beneath it, the squeaks of wheels against the tracks as the train reached the turn began to sound. And finally Sheila seemed to understand. She moved down the stairs, tentatively at first and then with greater speed as she got lower and heard the approaching train. She reached the turnstile and vaulted over. I turned and ran back toward the track.

The headlights were brilliant in the tunnel; the train was about to round the turn.

I reached the edge of the platform and waved my hands, shouting at the top of my lungs, just as the train burst into sight and came barreling into the station. For a brief moment I saw the con-ductor - driver? What do they call those guys on subways anyway? - as he approached. He gave me a look that someone reserves for an idiot, and then he was gone, out of my sight as the train sped past. He never even applied the brakes.

The train sped off to the north, the red tail lights first bright but steadily dimming as it sped away, and I lowered my arms. I realized I was still shouting and stopped. It would alert the bunny monster. Not that it needed alerting, but still...

"Son of a bitch."

Sheila stood next to me, watching the train speed away with despair in her voice. I glanced toward her and saw it on her face as well.

"Come on," I said. "We're getting out of here."

I grabbed her hand - she did not try to pull away - and led her toward the northbound tunnel at the end of the platform. I swore under my breath when we reached it. There was not a service walkway, like I thought there would be. Would there even be one further down?

"You've got to be kidding." Sheila pulled back then, removing her hand from my grasp as she shook her head in denial. "You want to walk down the tracks."

"Better than waiting here for that thing to get its act together."

"We're waiting for the cops."

"Are you really sure they will get here first?"

Just then a loud thump echoed through the station. It came from the direction of that concessions cart. A cold spike of terror surged through me, and I could see from her expression that Sheila felt the same.

"No choice," I said, and held out my hand to her.

She looked back over her shoulder toward the turnstiles and the stairs leading up, then swallowed and took a deep breath. Then she nodded to herself and took my hand.

Together we hopped down from the platform onto the tracks and ran northward, into the darkness of the subway tunnel.

———

I've seen movies and shows where people creep down dark tunnels, whether subway lines or roads or just plain old walking tunnels. In those shows the light continues for a long time, and even after they round the corner from the light source they can still see, however dimly.

That is not at all how it is in real life.

Within ten paces I had a hard time making out details on anything except for the subway rails themselves. Ten paces further on we came to a bend in the tunnel, and I could barely see anything. The thought of the bunny monster lurking behind us, or just as bad a train running up on us from behind, compelled me to keep running, though. So I did.

And within two steps, I tripped over a rail tie and fell headfirst to the ground.

My chin struck the edge of a tie as I landed and I felt a searing pain as my skin tore. I could not see it, but I knew I was bleeding. Badly.

I lay there for a long several seconds, clutching my bleeding, throbbing chin in my hand. Beside me, I heard Sheila panting heavily, sucking in great quantities of air as quickly as she could. I envisioned her bent over, hands on her knees as she tried to regain her breath, but in the darkness she was just one shadow on top of fifty more.

"Are you ok?" she asked between breaths.

Trying to ignore the metallic taste in my mouth - I may have bitten my tongue as well, though it was hard to tell, as ubiquitous as the pain was right that minute - I coughed and nodded.

"Great," was all I could manage, but it seemed

to be enough. She took a deeper breath and I could almost hear her relief as she took my hand and helped me up to my feet.

I looked around and was surprised that I could just barely make out some details. A dim green glow came from ahead, around the corner. I had not noticed it before; my eyes must have been beginning to adjust to the gloom, but it was still hard to make out anything more than the curve of the rails and the outline of Sheila's body.

There was nothing for it but to continue on, so we did, more slowly this time. I tried not to reduce us to a crawl, but after that fall I found myself gingerly testing each foothold before shifting my weight ahead, to make sure my foot was on a good surface and not in a pit or on the edge of a tie. It made for slow going. Much slower than was wise in our circumstances, but I could not complain. Sheila did not either.

Eventually we rounded the corner and were rewarded with light that was bright enough to make out the tunnel in detail. It came from a small lamp that looked like one of the stoplights you can see at most street corners. A quick look at it revealed why: it *was* one of those stoplights. Except it only had red and green, not yellow. Right then, the green light was the only one lit.

I cast about quickly and found what I was looking for. Through a gap in the wall to the left, a gap which led to the southbound track I was sure, I saw a small metal scaffold running along the wall. At last, there lay safety. Of a sort.

I felt my spirits buoy as I strode over to the gap and peeked through.

Looking right, all was blackness except for a

dull glow a ways down the tunnel, although right there the glow was red. Probably to signal the proximity of the station and that the conductor needed to begin stopping the train. Although, with the station closed what would be the point?

Regardless, there was no train coming and the scaffold lay just past the southbound rails. The only problem was a lack of stairs or ladder leading up to it.

"That's you plan?" Sheila said.

I glanced aside at her and saw that she was nodding in approval, a hopeful gleam in her eyes. She no doubt thought as I did, that there had to be a maintenance access between stations. Some of them were miles apart, after all. And if that were the case, the access would almost certainly link up with the scaffold. At the very least, the scaffold would make for much better footing, and safer, than walking the rails. And best of all, the scaffold was lit by dim blue-white lights in fixtures that were set in the side of the tunnel at regular intervals. We would be able to see better as well.

I nodded. "We just need to find a ladder up."

Sheila sniffed and darted forward, hopping over the rails - missing the third rail by less than an inch - until she stood below the scaffold. Then she bent her legs double and jumped straight up. My jaw, pained as it was, fell open in astonishment. She must have pushed herself a good three or four feet off the ground, if not more. She grabbed the middle bar making up the guardrail at the scaffold's edge. There she hung for a second before she swung her legs up onto the walkway. She then shimmied the rest of the way on and rolled to her feet.

I just stood there, feeling like an idiot and no doubt looking far worse.

She just grinned back. "I was on the varsity gymnastics team."

All sorts of possibilities that were extremely inappropriate in that particular situation sprang to mind, unbidden. "Well," I said, clearing my throat and forcing those thoughts away, "give me a hand up?"

Sheila's grin became positively impish.

A few moments later, after much huffing and puffing and with a good deal of help from Sheila, I managed to haul myself up onto the scaffold.

That really sucked. But it sure beat walking the rails.

I got to my feet and we got moving, our pace a lot better now that we had sure footing. Things were looking up, and I began to think we might actually get out of this with our skins mostly intact.

So naturally, that was the precise moment when everything went right to hell.

———

The roar came immediately after the thud. And by thud, I mean more like an earth-shaking kaboom than the everyday thud of dropping a sack of potatoes. It was *loud*.

Problem is, the roar was even louder. And it was not some incoherent bellow. No, it was a single word - my name. My name, spoken with all the fury of a hundred, no make that a thousand, women scorned. It was enough to almost make me fall over dead from shock and terror.

How I managed not too was beyond me. Maybe it was Sheila's presence, her eyes widening in fear that I knew mirrored my own. Or maybe it was a determination that I did not even know I had. Regardless, after staggering for a moment before the onslaught of sheer volume, I looked back down the tunnel toward the station we had fled and, seeing something big moving in the shadows of the tunnel back there, I did what any red-blooded man in the prime of his youth would do in that situation.

I ran like hell.

I pushed Sheila ahead of me and just ran, thanking the good Lord that we had made it onto the steady footing of the scaffold before the bunny monster decided to get its act together.

Of course, from what I had seen when I looked back, bunny monster was probably the wrong term to use; the thing looked much larger than it had been, if the shadows were a good indicator of its size. But there was no time to dwell on that, not if we wanted to have a prayer of getting out of there.

So we ran, fast as we could.

Sheila impressed me right off. She needed no coaxing; she was off like a gazelle, running far faster than she had on the streets above. I can only assume the full understanding of what we were facing moved her to new levels of effort. Or she was not really giving it her all before. Either way, it was all I could do to keep up with her, and I'm no slouch in the running department. Or at least, I wasn't, back in the day. But as I panted and struggled to keep up, I found myself tallying up the number of years that had passed since I ran track in High School. It was a depressingly large number.

I did not have time to consider that number for very long.

Something struck me from behind in the center of my back, and I fell forward. I threw my hands out to lessen the impact of the fall, but all the same I once again struck my chin against the floor. This time, spots of light flashed across my vision and an intense ringing filled my ears. I literally lost track of everything that was going on around me, intense as the impact, and the pain, was.

Somewhere in the background, I heard Sheila scream.

A voice - a very loud voice - in my mind screamed at me to get up. Get up now, or I was a dead man, and likely Sheila would die as well. Normally a compelling argument, but I found I could not make my limbs move, at least not in a coherent manner.

Gradually the stars in my vision and the ringing in my ears began to recede and I became more aware of the environment around me.

I really wished I had not.

My back felt wet and sticky where whatever it was that struck me made contact, but there was nothing and no one else in the immediate vicinity besides Sheila.

However, somewhere not too far off, something large was moving down the scaffold toward me. The scaffold creaked and groaned with its every step, but still it kept coming. Sheila was crouched next to me, shouting at me to get up, to move. She held on to my right hand with both of hers and she was pulling frantically at me, trying to help me up.

I went with the force of Sheila's tug and rose to a sitting position. There I stopped as the monster strode into view. In fairness, it more hopped than walked. That much, at least, it kept of the bunny persona the beast had been wearing. Aside from that, though...

Its head was hideous, a twisting of the cute bunny face it had worn into something vile, hungry, vicious. Its snout was short, with an upturned nose, but its forehead rose quite a bit higher than the bunny's had. It bled slowly from a gash on its left temple; that must have been where the majority of Sheila's blows had landed, back in the station.

The rest of its body was...the best word that comes to mind is bloated. It was as though the bunny's body had expanded like a balloon until it reached the size of a german shepherd and then cracked in multiple locations as its skin stretched beyond the breaking point, leaving areas where it was covered by soft-looking white fur and other areas that were black, or maybe very dark green, and scaly. Ooze of some sort or other dripped from those scaly parts; where it fell to the metal walkway of the scaffold, a soft hissing issued and steam, or a mist of some sort of gas, wafted up. The analytical part of my brain put two and two together and realized that the ooze, whatever it was, was acidic.

The worst part, though, were the thing's eyes. They were different from when it wore the bunny mask. Still slitted, red, and piercing, but somehow now the red was that much redder and they almost seemed to glow with a burning light of their own. It gazed at us - at me - and I could see its rage, towering like the skyscrapers in the city above us.

All at once, the mental pressure that it had used on me all those times to force me to its will came crashing down. But it was stronger, so much stronger, than it ever had been before. My hands flew to my temples and I heard myself crying out as I fell backwards. Pain, far worse than any physical pain it had inflicted with its claws all those times, ran through every fiber of my being, down through to the depths of my soul.

Fool. To think you could beat me.

I thrashed around, mindful of nothing but the pain and the booming voice of the bunny monster in my mind.

I would have left you for last, as a reward for your service. Ended you quickly. But now...

The pressure redoubled and the world began to fade beneath a red haze that filled my vision. It was too much. I was going to pass out, and then it would finish me while I was unconscious. I know I screamed. I must have. But no sound reached my ears except the thumping of my heart and the gleeful mental cackle from my foe.

And then I blacked out.

———

Blacked out is not the right term.

I lost track of what was going on around me as the pain overwhelmed it all. By all rights, I should have fallen unconscious as my mind sought a last refuge from the bunny monster's onslaught, one last bit of peace before the end.

But that's not what happened.

Instead of the peace of oblivion, as my gaze filled with nothing but red and my mind registered nothing but pain, I blinked and found myself elsewhere. But not just elsewhere. Else*when.*

All at once, I found myself bathed in a soft, yet somehow sickly, white light and I realized I was standing upright. To my left and right stood walls that were painted a boring shade of pale grey. They stretched ahead, enclosing the corridor where I stood, for about twenty meters before bending sharply to the right. Looking behind me, I saw that the corridor did the same thing in that direction, except it bent to the left. Somewhere in my head, the analytical part of my mind took that in and decided that the corridor must double around itself to form a complete loop around a central core.

It all clicked together then. I was aboard Ketcham Station.

Of course, that made no sense. I had departed the station days ago, and it now lay adrift, uninhabitable, the victim of one of any of the thousands of stupendously unlikely, but deadly nonetheless, mishaps that could befall a space station. There was no way I could be on the station. I knew for a fact that I really lay on a scaffold in the southbound tunnel of the red line of Boston's T network, just two stops from Downtown Crossing. This was just...well, I did not know what it was.

But damn if it didn't seem real.

Voices echoed down the corridor toward me, and a moment later two men and a women, all dressed in lab coats with security badges on their left breast pockets, strode into view. The men were nameless faces to me, but I recognized the woman immediately as Dr. Liu, the researcher who had shooed me away earlier.

I didn't want to deal with her again, so I turned quickly back to the electrical panel I was working on. Then it hit me - I was working? I had not realized that at first, but then what else would I be doing? If this was not real, it must be a memory, and all I did on Ketcham was work. I presume.

The trio walked past me without slowing, though I thought I saw Dr. Liu cast a wary glance my way. They were discussing something in technicalese that was way over my head. I did not even bother to try listening, but then two words jumped out and grabbed me.

Quantum Tunneler.

Those two researchers in the cafeteria had used that phrase; one of the men flanking the Dr. Liu said it now. My interest piqued, I listened more closely.

"...the last test was very promising," the man, tall and lean with sandy-blond hair, was saying.

The other man, more dumpy and older, with a bad combover, snorted. "Promising? The damn rabbit came through in pieces."

"But it *did* come through. Horace and Shelby have high confidence that their adjustments are sound."

The balding man's responding snort contained entire levels of derision. "Really. And who checked their work? I would not trust those two to -"

"Enough!" Dr. Liu said in a stern tone, silencing both men. "We will proceed with the next test."

Baldy opened his mouth to protest, but she cut him off.

"As soon as you are satisfied with the adjustments, Leo."

They turned the corner then, and the rest of their conversation faded. Baldy's expression of chagrin as he vanished from sight spoke volumes, though. He had not planned on carrying that ball. Not one bit.

For the next several minutes, I finished up tightening the connections within the panel. It had gotten to the point that I could perform that particular job without paying much attention, so my thoughts began to wander. What was this tunneler thing? They were sending rabbits through it, whatever it was, and it was doing bad things to them. To put it mildly. But what *was* it?

———

Some time later, I turned a corner, dull grey and bland just like every other corridor on Kethcam Station, and found myself outside the lab where I first met Dr. Liu. The memory of our earlier meeting, and of her dismissal, flashed through my head and I almost turned around before anyone saw me.

Curiosity stopped me. What were they doing in there?

Through the viewing window, I saw a large group of the researchers clustered together, Dr. Liu among them. Stretch and Baldy were there also, Baldy looking resigned yet also intrigued. The two junior researchers I recalled from the cafeteria were there as well. They stood in front of a whiteboard that was covered in greek letters and mathematical symbols that I found indecipherable, and were pointing excitedly to one part of the board in particular.

After a moment of discussion, Dr. Liu held up a hand and everyone stopped talking. Her lips moved and she looked to her left, where Baldy stood. He pursed his lips for several seconds while his eyes traced over the equations on the board. Then, finally, he nodded. I presumed whatever the cafeteria guys said, it had proven satisfactory.

Dr. Liu nodded and clapped her hands. The group dispersed quickly, each person going to a station around the room. They began throwing switches and making adjustments on equipment panels in the rapid, yet deliberate, way of people who were well practiced at their tasks.

A minute or so later, just as before, a man entered the room, but this time he only carried one cage. As before, when he grabbed the rabbit and lifted it out, the little creature struggled and kicked. But after a minute it settled down as the man set it down on a small black ramp that led toward the device in the back of the room that I could not see clearly last time.

This time I had no such difficulty.

The device took me by surprise. It was basically just a metal ring, about a meter in diameter, that rested atop a small table. It did not look like much of anything at all.

The ramp leading up to the ring began to move, and I could see that it was not a ramp after all; it was a conveyer belt. The bunny rode along placidly, chewing on some bit of food or other. I wondered if it was curious about the thing it was moving toward. Lord knows I was.

At that point, with the bunny about halfway to

the ring, I noticed the other device. It sat about three meters away from the first ring and looked identical to it in every respect, except that the conveyer belt was moving away from its ring.

I began to have a notion of what was going on. But it was too incredible, like science fiction.

Of course, I thought this while standing in a research lab on an orbiting space station with artificial gravity, so who was I to judge?

The rabbit neared the end of the conveyer belt into the first ring, and Dr. Liu gave an order. One of the junior researchers threw a switch and lights turned on around the circumference of both rings. The lights began rotating, slowly at first then more quickly, until, as the rabbit passed the threshold of the first ring, I could no longer make out the individual lights but only a ring of light superimposed upon each metallic ring.

The rabbit crossed into the first ring and there was a flash of brilliant white light along with a small gust of wind - I could see the researchers' hair suddenly whip to and fro - as well as a barely audible popping sound. It must have been much louder within the lab, for me to hear it outside.

A heartbeat later there was a similar flash of white light from the center of the second ring.

And then there was a tremendous explosion and a deafening roar. The researchers were knocked prone. Some lay still where they landed, others writhed in obvious pain. The plexiglass viewing window was cracked, the shockwave from the explosion was so strong.

I stood motionless, stunned. I knew I should have sounded an alarm, run for help, something. But the events inside the lab held me transfixed.

Smoke and flame leapt from the table where the second ring stood. Electrical arcs shot forth, followed by another roar.

And then, from within the billowing smoke, I saw a pair of eyes. Glowing red eyes with vertical slits, like a cat's.

———

I jerked awake, or back to reality at least, sitting bolt upright as the shock of the vivid recollection hit home.

The bunny monster. It was the bunny monster's eyes I saw through the smoke on Ketcham Station. Dr. Liu and her associates *created* the bunny monster. Not intentionally, to be sure. But whatever they were doing with those rings - I had to assume it was some sort of teleportation device - changed that rabbit, made it into something...different. Something twisted.

And then Sheila pulled at me again and I remembered the situation I was actually in. The bunny monster, hugely grown now from what it had been at first, was approaching steadily, its eyes narrowed as it focused in completely on me.

"Get up!" Sheila shouted, and I wasted no time in obeying.

For a brief moment, I considered how to fight against the bunny monster. But then it roared again and I realized the futility of that thought. So instead, once again, we ran.

Fast.

It was only after I had put a couple dozen running steps behind me that I realized the crushing pressure that I had felt in mind my just moments ago - was it even that long? - was gone. I risked a glance over my shoulder. The bunny monster was still there, still coming. It's eyes still burned with fury, a fury that was directed at me with a fierce intensity.

And yet I suddenly felt nothing.

No, that wasn't right. I felt it, but its was somehow not as mind-crushing as it had been before. Because of what I had remembered?

I slowed, then stopped, and turned to face the monster.

"Barry, what are you doing? Run!"

Sheila's voice boomed in my ears, but at the same time it was like I was listening to her from within a glass bubble - the words came through but they were stepped down, slower and deeper than normal. Almost stretched out.

In the depths of my mind I heard another voice, also muffled and muted, raging at me and trying to force me to bend. To break. It was the bunny monster, that much was certain. But it was as though the beast had lost its power, or something was shielding me from it. Something strong.

Whatever mental strength or protection had manifested itself within me just then, it obviously did not offer physical protection as well. What trick of the mind ever did? But even knowing that, I found I could not turn away and run, no matter the urging of my mind. I stood tall and stared it in the eye as it advanced, and found, somehow, that I was smiling.

"You are an ugly bastard under all that fur," I said.

I did not say it particularly loudly. Hell, I did not even say it in my normal speaking volume. But the words cut through the air between us like a knife, the sound seeming almost deafening to me for a second.

The bunny monster reacted even more strongly. My words struck it and it recoiled, its eyes widening. In pain? Anger? Confusion? All of those? More?

Whatever the reason, it stopped its advance. In the brief respite I made a waving gesture with my hand toward Sheila. I silently willed her to take the hint and run, get away, while I ran interference here. And for a moment, I thought she did. Then a movement to the side drew my gaze and I saw her standing to my left, her jaw set determinedly despite the fact that she was visibly trembling. My heart sank even as my mind shouted her praises, both for staying to assist against the beast and for her composure in fighting back her fear.

The bunny monster growled and I looked back at it. It had drawn back on itself, crouching like a cat ready to spring at us. Which was a neat trick, since it still resembled a bunny, at least partially.

"Fools," it said softly. But again, soft as its words were, they reached my ears without difficulty. "I have seen a million of your worlds begin and end, watched the turning of ages unnumbered. *You* would stand against *me*?" A deep, rumbling chuckle, fill with mockery, issued from it.

"What are you?"

Sheila asked what I had been wondering for days. But I already knew the answer before the bunny monster replied. It came to me in a flash, an insight that blossomed seemingly from nowhere. I can only assume it grew out of my sudden recollection of the events on the station. I told myself that was all it was; the alternative, that it had come from...elsewhere...was too unnerving to think of.

The bunny monster was not just a warping of that poor rabbit by the teleportation process. No, in making their teleporter, Dr. Liu's team had torn a hole in reality, a hole with no distance, as we know it, between one side of it and the other, even though those sides in fact stood several meters apart. But creatures inhabit that world between the sides, between what we call space. The monster had taken the rabbit the way superstitious people used to believe a demon could take possession of a person. Now it was revealing itself. Maybe it really was what those people called a demon. And now it was prepared to give birth to its progeny, a progeny that would be at home in our world, not in the spaces between. And that would spell the end. For many people, certainly, and maybe for everyone and everything.

We could not let that happen, Sheila and I. Glancing at her again, I saw that she did not understand the way I did. But she could see it was an abomination, and for whatever reason if I was not going to flee it, neither was she. Her jaw, already set, firmed even more and her eyes narrowed in concentration.

The bunny monster spoke again, and its words were a call to battle if ever I had heard one. Not that I *had* ever heard one. But they seemed to fit, regardless.

"I am your death."

———

The bunny monster advanced, its maw opening

wide to reveal an expanse of teeth. Big, sharp, pointy teeth by the dozen. It growled, and its breath was hot on my face even though it was still several meters away. Right then, my earlier question sprang to mind: how do you kill a vampire?

And I knew that was the wrong question. The same way I suddenly understood what the monster was and where it came from.

"It's not a vampire," I said to myself. "It's a *demon*. How do you kill a demon?"

"You don't," Sheila said, and I realized I had spoken more loudly than I thought. Reaching into her purse - it suddenly struck me how wonderfully feminine it was that, through all that had gone on since we bumped into each other on the streets above, she kept ahold of her purse - and pulled out a beaded chain that she wrapped around her right hand. "You banish it."

Sheila stepped forward to meet the bunny monster, her hand raised high, and I could see a small metal cross dangling from the end of that chain.

A rosary. She carried a *rosary*? Who carries a rosary anymore?

How many people even *know* what a rosary is anymore, dude, replied that annoying voice in my head that always told me when I was being a dummy.

"Be gone, beast," Sheila said in a firm voice of authority. Authority, and...faith.

She was a believer.

The bunny monster stopped for a moment. I could swear it was perplexed as it considered her and the small little cross dangling from her hand.

Then it began to chuckle. Slowly at first, then

with greater gusto until its chuckle became a laugh and then a full-on guffaw. It was quite rude, actually. Sheila was not being funny at all. In fact, the more I thought on it, the more I realized she had the right of it.

I stepped up next to her and placed my left hand overtop her right. If she could believe, I could too. Hell, after everything that had happened and all that I had learned I could not *not* believe.

Scowling, I said in as firm and commanding a tone as I could muster, "Be gone!"

The monster just laughed harder. And it advanced. It was not moving quickly; it's bulk prevented very quick movements on the walkway, narrow as it was.

Wait. That did not make any sense. The thing had moved quite well just a moment or two ago, and the walkway was not any narrower than it had been. What the hell?

It was growing.

Son of a bitch, it was growing, expanding even further than it already had. Especially around its belly, where its babies were surely about ready to burst forth. The patches of fur were smaller now, more stretched. The oozing, scaly areas larger. Greater amounts of that ooze dripped off the bunny monster's bulk. One particular drop caught my eye as it pooled at the bend of its left foreleg for a couple seconds before dropping away.

My gaze followed the drop as it fell. I watched as it hit the metal of the walkway floor. And as it bubbled and hissed as wisps of gas rose from the spot where the drop landed.

Acid. The ooze was acid. I had noticed that before, but it had not clicked. I looked at the metal plating at the monster's feet. A few meters back, where it had paused last, several small holes were eaten through the walkway. The monster was moving now, though, and the drops did not have time to pool.

But it was also larger, and oozing more.

I squeezed Sheila's hand, a plan forming in my mind. She winced slightly and shot a glare my way. I nodded toward the floor and her eyes followed the motion of my head. They widened. She understood.

Together, we stepped forward, toward the monster which now crouched only three meters away.

"Be Gone!" I shouted, and I heard her shout it as well. Our words rang out in unison, amplifying each other as the sudden hope and resolve I felt seemed to give them strength.

Then, suddenly, the little cross dangling from our hands flashed. Just a little flash of light, but I saw it, plain as day.

The bunny monster stopped. Its eyes grew wide and its jaw dropped open, but not in a roar or in a show of intimidation. In amazement.

In fear.

"You know Him?" It said, its voice, so strong and mocking a few seconds earlier, now quivering and uncertain. "Impossible! You cannot -"

I moved forward again, and Sheila came with me. She needed no prompting; it was as though we both knew what we needed to do without discussing it with each other. Like our minds were one, just then.

"Be Gone," we shouted in unison, and the cross lit up again, brighter this time.

The bunny monster drew back, open fear on its face as it retreated. The ooze was dropping even faster now, almost a steady stream of the stuff.

The light from the cross remained; it even grew brighter. In fact the entire tunnel seemed as though it was becoming illuminated by it.

Then I heard the noise behind us and I realized it was not the cross that was glowing. It was reflecting the lights of the southbound train as it approached from further up the tunnel.

The beast noticed the train as well and its eyes narrowed once more. The fear lessened on its face, and it grinned for a second.

"Well played," it said, and it placed its foot down on the bit of walkway it had just abandoned in its retreat.

With a loud squeal of protest, the walkway, having reached the edge of its endurance between the beast's weight and the corrosion caused by its acidic ooze, gave way, its outer edge collapsing downward until it struck the floor of the tunnel, leaving a ramp where a minute before there was flat walking space.

The beast's eyes widened again as it tried to prevent itself from falling, and for the briefest of moments it appeared the bunny monster might succeed. But slowly, ponderously, it lost its balance and toppled down onto the floor of the tunnel.

The bunny monster rolled over as it fell, its momentum carrying it clear of the walkway wreckage. I heard the horn of the train sound as the conductor saw what happened - Lord knew what he thought of it. Then there was a flash of white-blue light as the bunny monster struck the third rail, the one that carried the electric current for the trains.

Brakes squealed, but even louder squealed the bunny monster.

And then the train barreled over it, its momentum too much to prevent a collision.

The front car lurched, bouncing off the tracks and slamming into the pillars dividing the southbound from the northbound rails. But the momentum of the cars behind it kept pushing the train along. Unable to leave the rails completely because of the narrowness of the tunnel, it ricocheted from one side to the other, rending the walkway to the south of us and the pillars on the other side, shattering train car windows, tearing open the metal of the cars' sides until finally it came to rest with the front car, battered and crushed, halfway out into the station to the south.

———

At some point during the crash, I threw myself atop Sheila and bore her down onto the walkway in a show of stupidity and chivalry. Chivalry because, hey she was a lady and men protect ladies. Stupidity because...duh I'm going to protect her from a train wreck with *my* skinny ass?

Regardless, it worked. As the dust settled and emergency lights kicked on - many of the nearby illuminations were either shorted out or flat-out crushed by the crash - I took stock of our situation and was gratified to find that neither she nor I were hurt. Or at least, no more hurt than we were already.

"Holy shit," Sheila breathed as I helped her to her feet.

"No kidding."

We looked down the tunnel at the wreck and I could not help but be impressed.

Then I heard groans and weeping from the passengers in the train and my moment of awe turned into sickness, guilt. People were hurt and we had caused it.

I had caused it.

"This is all my fault," I said, and I collapsed down onto my knees.

"Bullshit," Sheila said as she crouched down next to me. "It was that thing's fault."

She was right, of course, but that did not make it any easier to accept the fact. I think I might have shrugged. Or maybe I just shuddered. Regardless, I was unable to stand back up for a good minute or two. I just crouched there, looking at the destruction in the tunnel and feeling miserable.

Sheila lurched me back to reality. "Do you think it's dead?"

"What?"

She looked at me like I was an idiot. "It survived being run over by a truck and being brained."

I snorted and, finally, pushed myself back up to my feet. "It's a demon. You don't kill demons, you banish them, right?"

She flushed and looked away. "It just seemed right." She drew a breath, then added, hastily, "I don't really believe in that stuff." She sounded like she was trying to convince herself as much as me.

I quirked an eyebrow at her and pointed at the rosary, which was still wrapped around her hand.

"Family heirloom," Sheila said. Then she cleared her throat. "Come on."

She walked over to the break in the walkway and, keeping three points of contact, lowered herself down the newly-made ramp until she reached the tunnel floor. Then she looked back up at me, expectantly.

"You coming?"

I actually had no intention of going down there. The smart thing to do would be to high-tail it north on the walkway to the next station, in case the bunny monster had survived. But then if it had died, or been banished or whatever, I would never know and I would spend the rest of my life looking over my shoulder for its return for no reason. On the other hand, if it was alive...

If it was alive, it was certainly injured at the least. This might be our best chance to finish it off.

I nodded and slid down, keeping contact with the ramp as Sheila had.

A moment later, we stood together between the rails and did not move. It was like we were rooted to the spot. Maybe it was because, up on the walkway, we were a bit more shielded from the real destruction of the crash. But down next to it, the debris thrown everywhere was all that much more real.

Or maybe we were both just re-thinking our decision.

None of that. I took Sheila's rosary-wrapped hand and smiled at her in a way that I hoped was reassuring. Then we stepped forward together to survey the scene and find the bunny monster.

———

It was like a scene from a nightmare.

The emergency lights only gave partial illumination, leaving most of the shattered train shrouded in shadow. Up ahead somewhere, a fire burned; not large, but enough to provide a flickering yellow-orange glow to the scene that was positively eerie. An occasional electric arc, from the third rail or from some shorted system within the train or in one of the shattered lighting assemblies in the tunnel, provided the final visual accent. The stench of ozone and dust filled the air, and above it a charred smell like rancid meat that had been left on a barbecue overnight.

And then there were the sounds of the passengers. Many more of them now that the initial shock had worn off. The groans and cries of the injured. The shouts and pleas for help from the panicked. And, in ones and twos, calmer voices from the few who had kept their wits about them and were trying to get the others organized, or at least to prevent them from panicking completely.

In all, Hollywood could not have done a better job if they were trying to make a scene to scare me out of my wits. Knowing that there really were injured people ahead, and maybe still the bunny monster itself, just made it worse.

I shivered, and not from cold; it was actually quite warm. Again I had the urge just to get back on the walkway and cruise north, away from the scene.

But I did not. Hand in hand with Sheila, I walked down the tunnel, hugging the gap between the southbound and northbound rails, since most of the train wreckage had ended up nearer the wall with the walkway. And besides, the third rail ran through that central area, and that was where we would find the bunny monster.

Slowly, carefully we picked our way over broken-off pieces of cement and metal, shattered plexiglass from the train's windows, and the occasional sign or lamp fitting that littered the ground. At one point we had to clamber over an entire wheel assembly that had broken off of one of the train cars.

That was where we saw the first body. An older man, in his late 50s probably, he was pinned beneath the wheel assembly, his face locked into an expression of surprise.

Sheila gasped and turned her head away. I found myself doing the same as sudden guilt rushed through me again. That guy would be alive if it wasn't for me. I knew it was a lie - it was the bunny monster's fault, not mine. It had crossed over to our world to wreak havoc, of its own accord. I did not ask it to, and for a while there I was all but helpless to stop it.

"At least he didn't suffer, looks like." Sheila looked up at me and squeezed my hand as she spoke, and I could tell she was dealing with some shadow of the same guilt I felt.

I nodded and inhaled deeply, and instantly regretted it as the growing stench of the scene filled my nostrils. Reminding myself to breath through my mouth, I said, "Let's move." I tried to sound determined; don't think I did very well at it.

But Sheila made no comment. She simply turned fully away from the man and led the way further forward along the train.

About twenty meters further, we found it: a great mass of charred and twisted flesh. Or rather, two masses of charred flesh. It had been cleaved in two by the impact with the train and obviously cooked by its contact with the third rail.

"This has to be the beast," Sheila said. The she coughed and bent over, making little heaves and clutching at her stomach.

I did not blame her. Here, the stench was almost overpowering. Even breathing through my mouth, it was like I could taste it. And that was without trying to talk. I pulled the tatters of my trench coat up over my chin so it covered my mouth and nose, but that did not help much at all. It truly, *truly* stank.

"Let's go back," I said as quickly as I could to avoid getting more of the stench than I had to. But Sheila shook her head.

"We have to be sure."

She straightened, getting herself back under control, and managed a half-smile that I returned, for all the good it would do with my mouth beneath my shirt. So I just shrugged, which earned a snorted half-laugh from her. Then we both took deep breaths and turned back to the burnt corpse of the bunny monster.

———

It was big. No shock there.

What was shocking was the fact that it appeared to be charred straight through to its center. There was no blood, not even from the areas that were cut off by the train. That made no sense at all. The third rail carries high voltage, but not enough to completely fry a mass of flesh as big as the bunny monster. Not in that short amount of time.

I frowned and looked around for a tool I could use. I found it a short while later - a hand rail that had been ripped off its mounts during the crash. It was about four feet long, and jagged at both ends. It wold make a handy spear.

I took the spear and walked up to the bunny monster's remains. I hesitated only for a second, then thrust the spear as far into it as I could.

The spear went in like a hot knife through butter, and then a large chunk of the remains simply broken off and crumbled into a pile of ash at my feet.

I stabbed it again, in a different location. Same effect.

"Looks like it's good and truly dead."

It was hard to argue with Sheila's logic, but after being terrorized by that thing for so long, that was not enough. The anger that I had kept bottled up where it could not find it, even with its psychic bond with me, the shame at being kept powerless, the guilt at being unable to prevent its atrocities... That anger demanded more.

I heard myself howling as I brought the metal pole down upon the remains of the bunny monster. Again and again I rained blows down, and each time another chunk lof its body fell apart and crumbled to dust. My arms and shoulders began to grow numb from the exertion, so different from what I normally asked them to do, but still I continued. Gradually, the anger gave way to a grim satisfaction.

That mother fucker was not getting back up from this.

Some time later - minutes, hours...seconds? - I reached a particularly bulky bit of char and brought my spear down. Like before, a big chunk of the bunny monster's remains broke off and crumbled. But this time something else fell out. A misshapen mass that at first was not anything I could recognize.

And then it moved.

It stuck an arm out and moved. It was certainly an arm because at the end of the limb as a hand, complete with an opposable thumb.

I stopped, dumbfounded, as the thing squirmed on the ground and the extended a second arm. And then first one leg, then another. Although I only recognized them as legs because of their location on the thing's body, down the torso from where the arms were. Aside from that, though... The arms and legs were the same length, as though the thing on the ground, whatever it was, was meant for walking on all fours.

I swallowed and looked at it more closely, where I presumed its head was. There was only an amorphous thing that might someday be a face of some sort on a stump that would probably contain a brain.

It was disgusting. Unnatural. Unlike any creature I had ever seen.

It was the bunny monster's child.

But it did not live long. Turns out, even though the bunny monster may have been a demon, its child was not. Or at least, not fully. I guess, having gestated here on earth, and having been nourished in the womb with human blood, it was bound by physical laws just like a human. Or maybe it was vulnerable because it had not been brought to term. Or it could not abide electricity.

For whatever reason, I found that a spear through the heart killed it just fine.

After that, Sheila found her own implement and joined me in breaking up the bunny monster's remains. It went without saying that we could not let any of its offspring survive. We found two more and dispatched them like the first.

———

It took a long time to get out of there.

Sooner than I expected, but longer than I had hoped, paramedics and other emergency crews showed up to take care of the train wreck. They came in through the station where Sheila and I had found ourselves trapped, and naturally they were not going to let anyone leave without giving them a clean bill of health.

Which was, frankly, ideal. And not just because I had several cuts on my arms and chest that required dressing, and perhaps a few stitches as well.

No, and I was ashamed to think this, the wreck made for ideal cover. Everyone was expected to be injured to some extent or another, and to have bedraggled clothing. No one asked Sheila and I if we were the people who had called asking for assistance in exiting the station earlier. The only focus was on treating the wounded.

And so I found myself sitting on a bench in the station, wincing as a paramedic applied alcohol to the smaller cuts on my legs and torso. My forearms, though, where the bunny monster had latched on so strongly...

"You're going to need stitches, buddy," the guy said as he pulled off the makeshift bandages Sheila had applied earlier. "A lot of them." He smiled apologetically then applied clean dressings to the wounds after applying antibiotic ointment.

"Where should I go?"

He shrugged and gestured toward the far side of the station, where a small gaggle of people with minor wounds sat or stood, waiting. "Just hang with those folks and we'll get you taken care of once we get the major trauma cases out of here."

That made sense, I suppose. Why tie up an ambulance with someone who was in no immediate danger when you could use it for a person who was going to die without help? And unfortunately there were a number of people from the train who met that description. For a moment, I was tempted to start beating myself up over that, but I forced my mind to other things.

Namely, Sheila. She waited on a bench by the gaggle of ambulatory patients, a few bandages recently applied where the bunny monster had dug into her. Thankfully not as many as I had. She smiled as I approached, and I pondered how quickly things changed. Not so long ago we were just faces on the street to each other. Me, a guy who might help her out with cash for the next meal. And her, a pretty but forgettable drifter, if only the bunny monster had not picked her out. But now, after the stress we had shared together, I felt close to her. Strange, considering I knew next to nothing about her.

Her smile said she felt the same.

I settled down next to her on the bench and let

out a long sigh. "I honestly didn't think we were going to make it through that," I said.

Sheila glanced sidelong at me and pursed her lips, but was silent for a while. When she finally spoke, it was in a subdued tone. "I never in a million years would have imagined something like that was possible." She shuddered slightly. "You could have just run away and let it take me." Her smile returned, and I could see the gratitude in her eyes. "Thank you."

Part of me felt good about that. Another part was insulted. Like I would just abandon someone to that thing's ministrations. But then, I reminded myself that I had pretty much done essentially that many times before encountering Sheila. So why was she different? Just because she was young, with a pretty face? I wanted to think there was something deeper to my decision-making process, but looking back on it, I was not sure.

But did it really matter?

Yes, said that inner voice that tended to annoy me so. Yes, it really does.

That was something that would take a long time to figure out. Fortunately, I had all the time in the world. So instead of waxing philosophical, I simply said, "You're welcome," and shook her hand.

I quickly wished I had not. Now that the adrenalin and stress of the incident had worn off, my arms really did hurt. I winced and let out a little groan as she squeezed my hand, and Sheila's eyes widened.

"Oh geez. I'm so sorry."

"No worries," I said through clenched teeth. "Dude said I need a bunch of stitches." I indicated the paramedic, who had moved on to a man who appeared to have a broken leg.

"You know," Sheila said, a mischievous twinkle in her eye, "there's a free clinic a few blocks from here. I'm on good terms with the manager, if you don't want to wait around for the ambulance crews to get back."

That was a great idea.

———

An hour later, I had fresh sutures in both arms, a new shirt and jacket on my back, a full antibiotic series and painkillers in hand, and a contented smile on my face. Sheila's medical friend had come through with flying colors. Even better, if anyone even noticed us leaving the T station they did not care. We were just another couple of people who were unlucky enough to get caught up in the wreckage, but also lucky enough to escape relatively uninjured.

Which was great, because having to answer questions about what we had been doing there would have been...awkward.

I stepped out of the clinic and waited on the sidewalk while Sheila thanked her friend again before following me out. During those few moments alone, I took in the street around the clinic. It was neither run down nor swanky, just sort of middling, with storefronts of all varieties and the usual cross-section of humanity walking, running, driving, or riding along in the late afternoon. The sun was low enough in the sky that it had sunk below the tops of the surrounding buildings, leaving the street in shadow. The sounds of hustle and bustle, the scent of cooking food, the perfume from a woman who brushed past me, the exhaust from the passing vehicles, and the chill of the breeze on my cheeks felt so much better than I ever recalled before. It was like it was all new, and I was noticing it for the first time.

I understood why: just a couple hours ago I thought sure I was going to die, and maybe many more people with me. Instead, I was alive. And it felt great.

Sheila pulled the clinic door closed and slid up next to me, linking her arm with mine. "Well, we've got a new lease on life. What do you want to do first?" The euphoria of having survived was hitting her as well, it seemed.

I shrugged. "I don't know. I shouldn't stay out too late, though. I've got work..."

I stopped, and not because of the incredulous look that appeared on Sheila's face. Something struck me then. She had mentioned it back on the train after I told her the story of what was going on. She thought everyone on Ketcham Station was dead. Hell, everyone on Ketcham Station *was* dead. Which meant...

I was dead.

I burst out laughing, and I felt all the worries and concerns that had been haunting me for weeks, hell months, maybe years, fly away with the sounds of my merriment.

"Hot damn," I said. "I'm dead."

Sheila looked askance at me. "Huh?"

"Everyone probably thinks I'm dead, killed up on Ketcham Station. Hell, I'm amazed they still haven't come and taken all my shit out of my apartment." Delighted, I looked at Sheila with a big grin. "I'm dead. I don't have to do a damn thing." Another thought struck me then. It was beautiful. Perfect, even. "Sheila, you said you were on the road?"

She nodded, still looking a bit confused by my sudden antics.

"Were you going anyplace in particular?"

Sheila shrugged. "Not really. Just seeing where the road takes me, experiencing the world."

My grin felt like it was going to split my face, as wide as it became. "Would you like a traveling companion?"

Sheila blinked, surprised. She was silent for several seconds, just looking at me and obviously thinking it through. Finally, she said, "Sure why not? Sounds like fun." Then she smiled again, and that smile contained the promise of freedom and happiness. Maybe not forever, but for a while. And that was good enough.

SUPPORTING PATRONAGE

Michael would like to invite you to become a supporting member of his website. Similar in concept to Patreon, a few dollars a month will give you access to exclusive content, and help him to focus more of his time to writing fun and exciting stories for your enjoyment.

Sign up at his website:

https://www.michaelkingswood.com/membership/
supporting-patronage/

ABOUT THE AUTHOR

Michael Kingswood is 20-year veteran of the US Navy submarine force and a lifelong fan of science fiction and fantasy literature. His work has appeared in numerous collections and anthologies, to include the Fiction River Anthology series from WMG publishing. He holds a bachelors degree in Mechanical Engineering as well as a Master of Engineering Management and a Master of Business Administration. He has four children and currently resides in San Diego.

Find Michael Kingswood online at:

www.michaelkingswood.com

www.facebook.com/michael.kingswood

https://steemit.com/@michaelkingswood

MORE BOOKS BY MICHAEL KINGSWOOD

GLIMMER VALE CHRONICLES

Glimmer Vale

Out-Dweller

Tollard's Peak

Robbed Blind

Wedding Gifts: A Glimmer Vale Chronicles Story

The Falconer's Stairs

Glimmer Vale Omnibus Edition #1

———

THE PERICLES CONSPIRACY

Passing In The Night

The Pericles Conspiracy

———

DAWN OF ENLIGHTENMENT

Masters Of The Sun

———

NOVELLAS

What Lurks Between

The Necromancer's Lair

The Champion

Veritas Morte

———

STORY COLLECTIONS

Tales Of Adventure #1

Tales Of Adventure #2

Short Story 10-Pack

A Jar Of Mixed Treats

———

SHORT FICTION

Michael has also published a number of shorter works,
links to which can be found on his website.